CRITICAL PRAISE FOR *DRAGON CHICA*

"It is very rare that a coming of age novel transcends its inherent limitations and attains the complex emotional resonance of adult fiction. *Dragon Chica* does this with great aplomb. The book explores with subtlety and depth the mature, universal issues of identity and connection, but it also retains its direct appeal to younger readers.

"May-lee Chai has performed a remarkable act of literary magic."

—Robert Olen Butler, Pulitzer Prize-winning author,
A Good Scent from a Strange Mountain

"Powerful, witty and profound, *Dragon Chica* introduces readers to a new kind of American heroine."

—Alicia Erian, *Towelhead*

"Eleven-year-old Nea has seen the very worst this world has to offer—from civil war in Cambodia, to the rice fields of the Khmer Rouge, to the bullying hallways of American public school. Thankfully, her heart and imagination bloom wide enough to let her continue longing for the best. As she grows into a woman, Nea navigates her difficult life with clear-eyed and courageous idealism. May-lee Chai has written a brilliant and important coming-of-age story about a young refugee who refuses to give up her search for that promised refuge.

"*Dragon Chica* is an important and deliciously readable novel that will hold you in thrall; you won't be able to look away from these pages, even as your eyes fill up with tears."

—Nina de Gramont,
Every Little Thing in the World and *Gossip of the Starlings*

"From the killing fields of Cambodia to a Chinese restaurant in the middle of the cornfields of Nebraska, *Dragon Chica* takes the reader deep into a compelling story about two sisters and the secret histories that surround them."

—Marie Myung-Ok Lee, *Somebody's Daughter*

CRITICAL PRAISE FOR *HAPA GIRL*

"I was captivated by May-lee Chai's *Hapa Girl* from the first sentence. It continued to be so powerful that I read it in one sitting. It's at once brutal and sad, humorous and plucky. Chai has beautifully captured the deep racism and bigotry that lurks in our country with how one misguided decision can change a family's fortunes forever. *Hapa Girl* made me think about the bonds of family and the vicissitudes of place long after I finished the last page."

—Lisa See, *Snow Flower* and *The Secret Fan*

"Easily labeled a coming-of-age story or a narrative about racial tensions in 1960s America, this memoir—whose title employs the Hawaiian word for mixed—is truly an homage to a loving marriage. Only the strongest kind of love could survive the crucible of a community hoping for a family's failure. Highly recommended . . ."

—*Library Journal*

CRITICAL PRAISE FOR
A GIRL FROM PURPLE MOUNTAIN
nominated for the National Book Award

"Gripping and historically grounded read"

—*Publishers Weekly*

"Tragic, funny, lyrical, and respectful, this intimate and unforgettable family chronicle is also a history of modern China."

—*Library Journal*

tiger girl

a novel by

MAY-LEE CHAI

GEMMA

Boston

First published by GemmaMedia in 2013.

GemmaMedia
230 Commercial Street
Boston, MA 02109 USA

www.gemmamedia.com

Printed in the United States of America

17   16   15   14   13   1   2   3   4   5

978-1-936846-45-0

Chai, May-Lee.
  Tiger Girl / May-lee Chai.
      pages cm
  ISBN 978-1-936846-45-0
1. Cambodians—United States—Fiction. 2. Refugees—United States—Fiction. 3. Self-realization in women—Fiction. 4. Family secrets—Fiction. 5. Women college students—Fiction. I. Title.
  PS3553.H2423T54 2013
  813'.54—dc23

                                          2013021807

Cover design by Howard Wong

CONTENTS

Contents

PART ONE

A mountain never has two tigers.

—traditional Cambodian proverb

CHAPTER 1

War Stories

"You're so lucky," Ma said to me, the highway straight as a ruler's edge, the fields dense and green, ripe to be harvested. "Too bad you can't get good grades. You don't try hard enough. You're not stupid. You could do better."

It was August, just before the start of my sophomore year of college, and Ma was driving me back to school after a summer spent helping at the Palace, our family's restaurant.

I stared out the window at the blowing grass laid low in the ditches, the yellow-tasseled heads of the late summer corn whipping back and forth in frenzied waves. Darkening clouds lumbered across the sky like war elephants amassing on the border of some ancient battleground. Thunder rumbled, and I thought, Oh god, don't let it storm, no tornadoes, god not now, don't make us have to pull over in some shelter or, worse, have to spend the night in a Motel 6 like last spring. Not when I'm so close to making it through this summer without having another fight with my mother.

I didn't believe in any particular god, not in the rule-ridden god of the Baptists who'd sponsored us to come to America when I was eight, not in the blood-drenched god hanging on the cross in Sourdi's husband's church, not in the god of money whose three porcelain henchmen perched on the shrine in the back of Ma's restaurant. But I prayed to all of them now: god of weather, god of wind, god of mothers, god of Nebraska, hear my prayers. I clenched my fists so hard that my nails dug into my palms.

"I was a good student. I received a nineteen out of twenty on an essay in *français*." Ma pronounced it the French way. Frahn-say. "That's like an American A+. But the war was coming. My parents had to pay for my brothers' education."

"I thought you got married at sixteen?"

She ignored my interruption. "And then I had so many children. What chance did I have? I wanted to go to college and become a poet."

"I thought you always wanted to own your own restaurant and become a rich woman?"

"No. That was only after your father fell ill and we were so poor. I wanted to become an intellectual, but we couldn't afford it." Ma sighed. "I had to use my brother's copybooks. I had to trace their letters with my pencil, but I was a good student." She didn't add, *not lazy like you*, but I heard it in my head, her voice so disappointed because my GPA had fallen over the course of freshman year and I'd decided not to take any more pre-med classes and I wasn't going to become a doctor and be rich the way she'd hoped. "My teachers wanted me to go to lycée. They begged my parents to send me. They said I was a girl with potential."

"Good thing you didn't go. The Khmer Rouge would have killed you."

She inhaled sharply, and I knew I'd gone too far.

The heavens opened and rain fell like rocks. Giant goose-egg raindrops splattered across the windshield and battered the top of the car.

The world went gray, as though a light bulb had gone off in the sun.

Ma slowed to a near stop in the far left lane.

I craned my neck, wondering where all the trucks had gone, and tried to see if there was traffic coming our way.

Ma squinted her eyes, leaned forward so far that she could have rested her chin on the steering wheel, and eased the Honda to the shoulder. We crept forward, inch by inch, but it seemed as though the world were racing past us. Water poured down the middle of the highway, rushing toward the drainage ditches on either side. I watched as the rain beat the corn to the ground and the wind blew the rain in horizontal streaks across the windows.

As we sat on the shoulder, I thought, I could ask her now. Ask her about the lie. The lie that separated us. The lie that kept me tossing and turning at night and ruined my concentration during the day. The lie that she was my mother.

I wondered if maybe this storm was happening for a reason, but then I felt hokey and stupid and superstitious. I didn't believe in fate. Miracles, sure. The fact that we were alive at all was a miracle. But this storm's stranding me in the car with Ma felt less than miraculous. It felt like punishment.

The counselor at school had urged me to speak to my mother. "Be honest," she said. "If you're honest with your mother, then you can expect she'll be honest with you." A lovely sentiment, I thought, but she didn't know Ma.

My mouth felt very dry. My palms were sweaty. My throat felt tight.

The storm howled outside the car. Ma gripped the steering wheel as though she were the captain of a steamship, as though if she could just keep the wheel steady, we'd hold to our course, even as the world melted around us, swirling, as if we were being drained from a cosmic tub.

Then, abruptly, the rain ended. The wind hushed while the clouds seethed like molten lead, and for a moment I held my breath, searching the sky for signs of the copper-colored bruises that signaled a tornado was imminent, but the storm was moving on.

Ma and I sat silently side by side, watching the water in the ditches lap angrily at the edges of the highway.

Finally, a few rays of sunlight pierced the cloud cover and a truck zoomed down the road, splashing muddy water across our windshield.

Ma pulled back onto the interstate.

"I hope you'll study harder in school this year. I'm depending on you. You're the only one to go to college. You'll have to support the others when I'm gone."

It was like a miracle, I thought. As if Ma had a groove in her brain where she could set the needle so that she'd never skip a track. And I realized she'd probably been an excellent student indeed, far better than I, a kind of genius even. I must truly have been a great disappointment, the way my concentration could be broken by something as ephemeral as the weather.

And, like that, the moment was gone.

I knew I couldn't confront my mother then and ask her to tell me the truth, to explain to me why she hadn't told me before. Questioning my mother felt like questioning her love. I hadn't the nerve.

When I was eighteen, just before I left for college, my older sister, Sourdi, told me the truth. She explained to me that I'd been adopted, a wartime arrangement that was never meant to have been permanent. In 1975, as the Khmer Rouge were poised to take over Cambodia, my birth mother fell ill after her latest child, a son, was born. My father had fled the country, afraid for his life. He'd been associated with a faction in the government that was no longer in power. As the American war in Vietnam spread to Cambodia and Laos, as American bombs laid waste to the countryside and refugees flooded into the cities, the American-backed government of Lon Nol grew increasingly unpopular, and its ministers increasingly paranoid. They sensed potential threats from everywhere—from the Chinese merchants, whom they accused of being a fifth column for China; from those loyal to Prince Sihanouk, whom they suspected of plotting against them; from their own soldiers, whom they increasingly refused to arm.

Then, one day, soldiers came to the house, threatening to shoot my father, and my mother thought to shout, "Go ahead! Kill him! He's caused me nothing but trouble!" She complained that as a husband he was worthless. They used to be rich but now they were poor. What kind of life was this? She shouted loudly so everyone could hear, the soldiers, the servants, the neighbors. She wanted them to hear how much she hated her husband so they would think he was weak, not powerful, not someone who could overthrow a government. The soldiers left that day without shooting my father, but he knew he had to leave. Who knew when they'd come back? Who knew when they'd change their minds? My mother agreed, and my father fled in the night, promising to send for her and the children when he was safe and established in another country. He did not know, could not know, that the Khmer Rouge would take over the capital before he could send for my mother. No one believed Pol Pot could win. No one knew what he was planning.

Before the fall of Phnom Penh, my mother made a decision. She gave me, a precocious, talkative, energetic toddler, to her younger sister to take care of. She knew I enjoyed staying at my aunt's house, playing with my older cousin Sourdi. My aunt was energetic, her husband kind; they had gotten used to taking care of me while my mother had been recovering from the various illnesses that afflicted her.

Then, in the chaos of the Khmer Rouge takeover, I was evacuated with my aunt's family to the countryside. My mother and her sister were separated. They did not know how to find each other. My aunt raised me as her own, taught me to call her Ma the same as her children. She changed my name, calling me by my nickname, Neary, "gentle girl," and not Channary, "moon-faced girl," a fancy name for a different era. The Khmer Rouge were killing city people, the educated, the business classes, the Chinese, the Muslims, and then anyone they grew suspicious of—the pale-skinned, the myopic, the clever, the poor, the dark-skinned, the far-sighted. Eventually, I escaped with my aunt's family to a refugee camp in Thailand, never suspecting that the woman I called Ma was not really my mother, or that the siblings I grew up with were really my cousins.

I would not see my real mother and father again until I was eleven and living in Texas, where my family had been sponsored by a Baptist church to come to America. The rest of our extended family—grandparents, uncles, aunts, cousins—had all died as far as we knew.

One day we received a letter through the Red Cross: a man named Chhouen Suoheng was writing to Ma, saying he and his wife had been looking for her for years. Ma was overjoyed to discover that her older sister was alive and in America, but Sourdi was worried. I didn't know then that she knew these were my real parents and that she was afraid they were going to take me away.

After he found us, this man whom I called Uncle, just as Sourdi did, invited us to move in with him and his wife, to help them run "the family business," as he called it, a Chinese restaurant they'd purchased in a small town in Nebraska.

Our reunion was fraught with troubles. No one told me the truth. I called my birth mother Auntie, my father Uncle. Auntie was ill, suffering from PTSD and depression. She'd been wounded in the war, her face scarred beyond recognition. Once she'd been a beautiful woman; now her face was split in two by a long purple scar, dark on one side, shiny and light with scar tissue on the other. She was addicted to painkillers. She took too many antidepressants. Her moods varied with the drugs.

Worse, she didn't like the Americanized child I'd become. She found me rude and loud, nothing like the refined daughter she remembered. She blamed her sister for having raised me wrong. I had no idea why this woman stared at me so intently and criticized my every move. I had difficulty understanding her Khmer; she had difficulty understanding my English. She grew increasingly paranoid, certain Ma was having an affair with her husband, convinced they were planning to abandon her. She became obsessed with finding her oldest son, hoping he'd survived the Khmer Rouge. She set fire to the restaurant, lashing out at the people around her. Fortunately, the damage to the Palace was repairable. However, the damage to our family was not.

My father in desperation sold his stake in the restaurant and moved with her to Southern California, where they opened a donut shop and devoted themselves to tracking down their eldest son. But the trail ran cold, and my birth mother grew more depressed. She ended up overdosing when I was in high school. Suicide or accident, we'll never know. Despondent, wracked by guilt, honoring his wife's last wishes perhaps, my father broke all ties with our side of the family. We assumed he was still looking for his son.

I would never have known the true story behind the people I called Auntie and Uncle if Sourdi hadn't told me just before I left for college. She seemed to think it was a gift to tell me the truth.

Maybe I should have left well enough alone, but the truth had a way of sitting under my skin, like grit in an oyster. I wanted to rub it into a pearl, I wanted to expel this scratchy thing that kept me from feeling wholly myself.

I wanted to know why my father had rejected me. For that's how I saw Uncle's behavior. Because he had not claimed me as his own and asked for my return, I assumed he had not wanted me.

CHAPTER 2

The Apsaras Who Fell to Earth

Ma liked to tell me stories. When I was little, she complained that I was a naughty and difficult girl, noisy and precocious, the kind who refused to fall asleep. She would tell me stories late at night, trying to put me to sleep, trying to keep me from waking the other kids. With each story, I grew more alert. I tugged on her sleeve as she started to doze. I pinched the inside of her arm. "Tell me another story," I whispered. "Tell me more."

She told me stories about her own life—the big house she'd lived in as a child; her grandfather's Chinese restaurant, three stories high; her father, the teacher, who loved her so much that he killed every bug in the house before she went to bed just because they frightened her. When talking about the past made her too sad, she told me made-up stories. The dancing girl who fell in love with a man and lost her immortality, the monk who tried to ride a crocodile and drowned, the monkey who fell in love with a princess and was cast out of Heaven. In Ma's telling, her life mixed with ancient tales, and she became a heroine battling demons, a princess choosing among suitors, a goddess living among mortals.

The story of the Apsaras who fell to Earth was my favorite.

Once there was a dancing girl who defied Heaven's will and chose to live on Earth. She wasn't like her sisters. When she was born, rising fully formed from the Sea of Milk at the beginning of the universe, foam and salt still clinging to her ankles and her skin glistening wet, she did not cast her glance to the side, modest as a mouse. Instead she danced smiling, eyes shining; she wanted to see everything at once, taste everything. She couldn't keep her mouth shut; she couldn't keep her eyes open wide enough. Life in the Heavenly Palace, surrounded by the gods, bored her. She stared at the blue-green pearl in the sky and plotted her escape.

One night when the moon hid her face behind a cloud, the dancing girl stepped off the edge of Heaven and fell to Earth like a meteorite.

To earn her living, she danced barefoot on the sandstone floors of a temple, incense in her skirts, her earrings jangling like small bells. She danced as her sisters had taught her, as they had always danced in their palace at home in Heaven. No one had seen such grace before, her hands stroking the air like smoke, her hips swaying like a breeze. Soon men came from the four corners of the city, from all the provinces, from the twelve cardinal directions of the world, just to watch her dance.

She fell in love with a minor court official. She saw how he treated the servants, never losing his temper. She saw how he treated the elder courtiers, never losing his patience. He was shy, casting his glance downward, staring at the earth when she smiled at him. Later, when she danced for him, he blushed, but this time he did not look away. He looked into her face and said he loved her, would love her forever. Of course that was impossible, she knew, because she would live forever and the man would not. The dancing girl agreed to marry him without telling him her secret.

While her husband went to work in the king's court, the dancing girl passed her days in their modest home on the road to the temple. The monks came by every morning to beg for food, offering to earn merit for her family.

She smiled and gave them rice.

When her husband returned from court, she danced just for him in the light of the candles that flickered throughout their home.

They were very happy together, the man and the dancing girl.

But while she stayed young, the man grew older. His belly grew round, his skin became rough under her fingers, his black hair turned gray and then white, exposing the lumpy shape of his skull. She put her hands against his cool, dry skin, the mosquito nets drawn tight against the bedroll to protect his soft flesh. His breathing was labored now, so slow. One night she laid her hands against his forehead and knew his soul was ready to leave his body.

Before the man could take his last breath, though, she impulsively snatched his soul in the palm of her right hand. She was not supposed to intervene. The cycles of birth and rebirth were ordained by *dhamma*. But she flew away, high above the banyan trees. The roots dangling from the branches clawed the air, reaching for her skirts as she rode atop the wind as though it were a wave of water and flew safely through the night, home to the Palace.

Her sisters wept to see her; laughter was not strong enough to express their happiness. They gathered around her, pressing their palms together before their faces. They had thought she was gone forever.

But when the Lord Buddha discovered that she had brought a human soul to the Palace before its time, he was very disturbed, and called her before his lotus throne. She walked carefully in small steps, carrying her husband's soul tucked in her hand. The vermilion streamers before the altar flicked at her calves like the tongues of a dozen snakes.

She knelt to the floor and placed her forehead on the smooth stones. "Forgive me," she said. "But I love him. I cannot bear to be separated." And she cried with tears of pearls.

Her sisters wept again, now with fear and sorrow.

Then the Lord looked at her with compassion. Raising his right hand, he said, "Let it be so," and suddenly the dancing girl felt as though she were falling through the floor. The light of day went out like a candle flame snuffed between two fingers. Stars streaked by like strings of firecrackers popping as she fell backward into night.

When she awoke, she lay on a reed mat on a rough wooden floor, next to an old man who snored beneath his mosquito net. The wind blew through the open windows, carrying the sound of a river.

The dancing girl sat up slowly. She felt dizzy, a new sensation. She tried to climb to her feet, but found that her knees creaked, and her ankles were stiff. She rose only with difficulty. Pain was new for her. She tried to understand these feelings.

She walked around the tiny room, saw the small low table, the rough benches, the open windows. She saw that she was in a house on stilts at the edge of a brown river. Silver fish leapt against the current. Two oxen and a pig sniffed through the dirt below the floor in the blue light of the moon. The dancing girl felt a terrible pain in her stomach, as though a great hole were opening up from within. She knelt to the floor, clutching at her intestines. She cried out.

The old man woke with a start. "What happened?"

"I don't know," gasped the dancing girl. "I've never felt like this before." Suddenly her stomach growled with the sound of a tiger cub, and she shrieked. "Did you hear? There's a wild animal inside me!"

The old man laughed now. "You've had a dream, that's all. Why are you acting so foolish?" It was only her stomach growling, he said. And he told her it was time for her to make them breakfast.

After she had eaten a little and calmed her stomach, she stood up again and discovered that she felt a pressure inside her intestines. The old man explained that she had to go outside to relieve herself, so she climbed down the rungs of the rough wooden ladder, splinters pricking the soles of her feet. The smell of the pig and the oxen assaulted her nostrils immediately. The night wind swept around her, carrying terrifying sounds of laughing birds and chattering monkeys and roaring beasts. The pressure inside her did not abate, so she swallowed her fear and made her way through the tall reeds toward the bank of the river, where she squatted and was able to make the pressure go away.

Then the dancing girl stepped into the river to cool her feet. Splashing the soothing water against her skin, she leaned over the water and gasped. For there in the water looking up at her was the face of a very old woman with loose skin and missing teeth. The old woman stared at the dancing girl.

Finally, she understood what had happened to her.

She went back to the house and continued to live as a human being for many years, until her husband died. Then she wept bitterly. She shaved her head like a nun and rubbed ashes on her skin. Her sadness was like a pin in her heart, always pricking her; each hour now seemed a century long, each day an eternity. The sun shining in the sky did not make her happy and the stars at night offered no solace.

She had given up her immortality to be with the man she loved, but now he was gone anyway.

The children of the man and the dancing girl worried about their mother. They offered her delicious food to eat, soft noodles and boiled crabs and fine white rice. But she would only eat one bite before she sighed, "My food has no taste anymore," and she refused to eat another nibble. Finally, to ease her loneliness she began to speak her happy memories out loud. Each day when one of her children came to check on her, instead of eating, she told the child one of her memories. She continued this way for a hundred and twenty days, for she and the man had had many, many children. She described the way the man wrote with a fine hair brush dipped in black ink, the robes he wore when he went to court, the poetry he composed, the first time he'd seen her dance.

The children thought their mother had lost her mind. They remembered none of these things, these stories from the previous lifetime that the dancing girl had spent with her husband before she'd taken his soul to Heaven. The father they remembered was a poor peasant who'd never learned to write his name, let alone a poem.

Finally the dancing girl had no memories left to share, and she died. Her children burned incense for their mother and paid nuns to cry at her funeral, but nothing made them feel any better at all.

They were sitting together in the house of their parents, crying, when one son began to tell the story that his mother had told him. Then a daughter told another story. And they told the dancing girl's stories to each other all night long and all day. For four months they talked, until finally all her stories were told. While the children were talking, a seed took root in the remains of the dancing girl's fish pond. This seed grew into a giant tree as tall and as wide as a tree that had been growing for forty years. Then the children all bowed down before the miraculous tree and gave thanks to Buddha.

"That's not a good ending," I said, pinching my mother's elbow, trying to wake her.

She stirred, her eyelids fluttered.

"What really happened? What happened to the dancing girl and her children? She can't just die."

My mother smiled slightly and sleepily patted my leg with one hand. She fanned herself with the other, and the breeze brushed against my cheek like a kiss.

"Tell me," I whispered.

CHAPTER 3

The 108 Little Hells

Back in school for the fall semester of my sophomore year, I was haunted by dreams. I was a child again, lying in bed next to a woman who was telling me stories.

The light on the bed stand flickers—a power surge as a storm approaches on giant's feet. Lightning cracks the sky like an improperly fired kiln. My mother pulls the mosquito net close around us, creating a cocoon of gauze. The light glows distantly. I press my face into my mother's side, her nightgown smelling of jasmine oil, smoke and garlic, a hint of perfume. Her skin is smooth against my forehead. She strokes my arm absently.

The rain is coming. The air is thick with water, and sweat collects on both of us, mother and daughter, although we lie very, very still, waiting for the storm. Then my mother begins to tell her story, her voice softer than a whisper, a tickle in my ear.

I lean close, closer, trying to hear what she is saying, but her voice grows raspy, hoarse. I tug on her sleeve, I pull on her gown, but her voice turns to a growl, and I realize I've been tricked. This isn't my mother, it's a wild animal, a panther about to pounce.

I woke up in a sweat, my heart pounding, my sheets twisted around my waist. My roommate's snores thundered around me.

Lying in the dark, I watched the charcoal shapes of my dorm room gradually coalesce as my eyes adjusted to the moonlight slicing through the space beneath the shade and the windowsill, its blue light spilling through the shadows. I could see the edge of my desk, the top of my wooden chair, the soft lumpy outline of my roommate's bed, and the dresser with her ticking alarm clock atop it, the earring tree, and her framed family picture—everyone smiling with all their teeth exposed as they stand in matching ski outfits on a snowy mountain in California, taken when she was a child. I couldn't imagine my roommate's childhood. I couldn't imagine how she lived before she became this person farting softly and snoring loudly in the dark on the other side of the room. Her life seemed like something out of a TV movie.

I'd never realized such shiny people could actually live a flesh-and-blood life. My roommate Shannon was always cheerful. She drank regularly on weekends beginning Thursday late afternoon, she puked loudly in the women's bathroom, and then slept heavily, breathing acrid-smelling vomit breath into the air. She had the good grace not to ask me anything about my family after our first awkward conversations. I'd needed a roommate as my freshman roomies had decided to move off campus, and Shannon's roommate had ended up transferring to a different school, so we'd been paired in the room lottery.

Shannon had a steady boyfriend who played some kind of team sport, whose games she attended regularly. She'd shown me her albums of photos she'd brought to remind her of her wonderful family, her happy days in high school. *Here's me at prom, here I am at drama camp, this was my first boyfriend, this is me with my girlfriends on graduation.* If she lacked anything, it seemed to be an imagination, but that worked to my advantage. I didn't want a curious roommate. I didn't know how to explain my family to anyone, not even to myself. With Shannon, I could pretend that I too had the bland suburban life that she assumed was normal.

As I lay on my bed in the dark, as she snored like a giant, mouth open, I could not force my nightmare to recede and fade. If anything, each breath made the dream more vivid. The sound of the wind through an open window, lifting the edges of a white mosquito net. The mother reaching out her hand to touch my face. I flinched in my real bed in my dorm. My whole body shaking, I was suddenly cold.

I felt her hand against my skin.

Then I woke up a second time.

Night after night, I dreamed of my mother, not knowing which woman I was dreaming of.

In December, after months of this misery, I woke up in the middle of the night with a feeling like cobwebs around my heart and knew I had to do something. Better to confront the past, or it would keep haunting me.

And so I decided to visit Uncle. I had his last known address and the name of his donut shop.

I sold my textbooks, took my wages from my part-time job washing pots and pans in the school cafeteria, and bought a bus ticket to California to find my father. I had no idea what I'd tell him, what I'd accuse him of, what I'd ask him to do for me.

I didn't tell Sourdi. I told a story to Ma, said I wasn't able to come home for Christmas this year. Claimed I was going to spend winter break in California with my roommate. Shannon and I were applying to summer internships there, I said, and I'd have to stay for the interview. Her family said I could stay with them.

Like that, I lied to Ma, and she believed me.

Then I bought a long-distance bus ticket and left.

Riding the bus nonstop across the country, I was reminded of Ma's story about the 108 little hells. There were eight big hells,

she said, for souls that had committed really bad sins like mur-
der or rape, for monks who violated their orders by eating meat
or by starting families, obvious things like that. But for everyone else there were the little hells for all the sins that were just
bad enough, the ones you had to work off before you could be
reincarnated and try again to get life right.

"You mean everyone goes to Hell?" I asked. We were living in Texas in those days, and I was in elementary school. I
couldn't completely understand the Baptists yet, but I knew
they'd painted a different picture. "Doesn't anyone go to
Heaven?"

"Maybe saints," Ma conceded. "I don't know about Heaven.
But in the 108 little hells, there's room for everybody on Earth
in this life and the next and the next and the next after that."
Then she sighed to let me know that I was annoying her, that
I was the kind of daughter who was earning her own place in
one of the little hells right then and there. The Little Hell for
Unfilial Daughters Who Questioned Their Mothers' Wisdom.

Later we made a joke of it. Every time something went
wrong, we'd say which hell we'd landed in. When the car broke
down in the heat and we had to pull over and let the radiator
cool off while the traffic honked and sped past us, we were in
number twenty-eight, the Little Hell of Endless Car Repairs.
When the flurry of bills arrived at the end of every month,
number sixteen, the Little Hell of Too Little Money. When
the Church Ladies brought us another brick of cheese, it was
number 102, the Little Hell of Painful Farts. If we fought over
which TV channel to watch or which radio station to listen
to or which of us was supposed to take out the garbage, Ma
said she was in number five, the Little Hell of One Child Too
Many, which made each of us feel simultaneously guilty and
unwanted and jealous of each other. That was Ma's genius—
she turned guilt into a sibling competition.

Riding in the Greyhound, I leaned my head against the window and watched the flat desert plains of Utah pass by. The interstate seemed to have been built through the ugliest part of each state. Perhaps it was the only land cheap enough to build a highway on, I thought. There was no snow yet, only monotonous waves of sandy dirt. Then the batteries in my Walkman died, and I discovered that all the truck stops charged exorbitant amounts for AA batteries. Then, just as we entered Nevada, the toilet in the back of the bus overflowed. After our half-hour bathroom break in Vegas, one of the other passengers played two dollars in quarters at the slots and, in the final pull, won so much money that he said he could now afford to fly and bid us all adieu. Thing is, I'd played the same machine but had only allowed myself to spend a dollar. I had figured that luck would either be with me or it wouldn't. In that sense, I was right.

Number sixty-six, I thought. The Little Hell of a Long-Distance Bus Ride.

On the final leg of the trip, for the last five hours to California, I still couldn't sleep, even though I'd been traveling for well over twenty-four hours. I couldn't even concentrate to read the paperback I'd brought along. But as we entered California, the world began to change. Looking out the window as the bus lumbered along the highway, cars and trucks and trailers passing us by, I watched the scenery grow more lush as we emerged from the desert. I stared at the glaring green of the oleander shrubs and palm trees, the stoplight reds and yellows of the McDonald's arches, the billboards for Marie Callendar's and Shell stations. As we followed the sun westward, the shadows grew longer, stretching black and oily across the median like an inky tide chasing our wheels.

The world seemed too bright, too vivid. My heart began to beat too fast. I didn't want a panic attack to come on, not here, not now, so I closed my eyes and counted forward by fours to a hundred, then backward by sixes.

I always pictured the Little Hell for Ungrateful Daughters to be like the dark closet in the trailer that the First Baptist Church had rented for us. Ma locked me inside it once after a particularly heated argument. I no longer remembered how it started, but I remembered how it ended: with Ma dragging me by the arm and pushing me into the closet, the lock turning from the outside, a chair shoved against the knob just in case, although I didn't rattle it. I was too proud to try to escape. The whole time I was locked in the closet, I could tell exactly what my family was doing on the outside. I could smell Ma's cooking, hear Sourdi's laughter, listen to the cartoons on the TV, yet my family couldn't see me, couldn't hear me above their daily din. I'd never felt so lonely before, knowing my family could eat and laugh and watch Looney Tunes without me. I was like a hungry ghost at a family banquet, unable to partake of any human thing.

The whole episode probably lasted ninety minutes, two hours max. An eternity.

"How do you like that?" Ma asked finally, rapping on the door. "Are you ready to behave?"

"You're going to number ninety-nine, the Little Hell for Mean Mothers," I shouted through the door. "It's filled with mean old ladies, like the crazy lady across the street. And every day, she's going to come out and yell at you, 'Be quiet! Don't run on my lawn! Don't touch my dog!' Then you'll go back into your dark room that smells like medicine and bananas and—"

Ma surprised me then, throwing open the closet door. I expected her to drag me out and beat me, but instead she was laughing.

"Is that what you think? You're a funny kid. But maybe there's a small heaven for me when I'm old. I'd like my own place, all by myself, me and some mean old ladies with no kids to bother us."

Ma smiled, and I felt even worse than when she'd tried to lock me in the closet for eternity. To know that she could imagine a small heaven for herself and no place in it for me.

As the bus took the exit for Santa Bonita, I wondered if I weren't heading straight to the actual real-life little hell for ungrateful daughters, the one where I broke my mother's heart by looking for my father's family, the one where I acquired secrets I couldn't ever share.

It was possible, I thought, as I breathed in and counted backward, ninety-four, eighty-eight, eighty-two, seventy-six.

Possible, but also necessary.

I exhaled very slowly.

PART TWO

*In the water are alligators;
on the land are tigers.*

—traditional Cambodian proverb

CHAPTER 4

Uncle

The Santa Bonita bus station was small, a squat building with a dusty Christmas wreath nailed over the doorway. I walked across the asphalt, hitching my backpack over my left shoulder as I followed the other passengers. The light in California was different from that in Nebraska, yet it seemed oddly familiar. And then I remembered this feeling of entering a bright but unknown world. When we first arrived in Texas, coming off the plane to the refugee processing center in Houston, I held on to my older sister Sourdi's hand so tightly that she pinched my arm to make me stop. I tapped my feet on the asphalt, amazed by the springiness of the black tarry ground beneath my sandals, and Ma told me to stop behaving like a monkey. I was embarrassing her. If I misbehaved, she said, the Americans might send us back.

After that, I walked very carefully, stepping in Sourdi's shadow all the way across the tarmac.

Such a long time ago.

Before I left, I'd written a letter to Uncle, telling him I was coming to see him in California. After I bought my bus ticket, I called his donut shop from the phone in the hallway of my dorm. Some woman had answered and I'd told her to give my uncle a message: his niece was coming to visit for winter break. "Be sure to tell my uncle when I'm arriving," I'd said. But Uncle hadn't called me back and I left without knowing if he'd be happy to see me, or if he'd even meet me at the station.

Stepping from the sunlight into the shadowy interior of the bus terminal, I found myself straining to see as I scanned the empty rows of orange plastic seats, the straggly line at the newsstand, the families gathered in awkward clumps beneath a giant green plastic Christmas wreath and a drooping "Happy Holidays" banner. A few children carrying metallic helium balloons chased each other, whooping and shrieking as they wove their way around the arriving passengers. A young blond woman squealed and threw her arms around the thick neck of a soldier in camouflage. The soldier dropped his duffel bag and swung the woman around like the world's largest toddler. Then I noticed the older Asian man standing by the wall under the giant sign with the bus schedules marked in block letters. He was staring anxiously at the passengers filing into the station.

I recognized Uncle immediately, although it had been almost eight years since we'd last seen each other. He didn't look as old as I remembered, even though he had to be in his late fifties by now. He still had the prominent cheekbones, the burnished, coppery skin, and the thinning hair, but he'd filled out—he wasn't half as skinny as he used to be. He stood straight, shoulders back, holding himself with the posture that had been drilled into him by the nuns in his Catholic lycée in Phnom Penh before the war. He was the only Cambodian man in the station.

Uncle was staring past me at the line of people emerging through the door. I walked right up to him.

"Uncle," I said, politely. "It's me. Nea."

He startled and stared. I wondered if it was my hair; I'd tried streaking it blue in the dorm earlier in the semester, but the home kit hadn't quite worked out. Or if it was that he didn't recognize me because I no longer looked like my twelve-year-old self.

"You've grown so much," he said after a pause.

"Ma always said I ate like a boy."

Uncle nodded and turned away quickly, as though he couldn't bear to look at me. "I'm parked out front. Follow me."

He didn't even ask me why I'd come, I noted. Whether that was a good or bad sign, I did not know.

As we walked across the parking lot, I had to peel off my winter coat.

Uncle wiped at his face with a handkerchief, then folded it neatly and placed it back in his pocket. He stopped at a dusty Toyota and opened the trunk for me to put my backpack inside. Finally Uncle spoke. "I was so surprised. You look so much like her when she was young." He wiped his face on the back of his hand. We both pretended it was just sweat he was wiping away. "You look just like my wife. When she was young, I mean. Before the war."

The woman I'd met had her face divided in two by a long purple scar, one half dark from the scar tissue, the other too light. Auntie had tried to blend the two halves together with makeup, but I could always tell. I'd once seen a picture of Auntie, my mother, from before the war, before Pol Pot took over, before the minefields took their toll. She'd looked young and beautiful and happy. Nothing like the woman I'd known. She'd also looked glamorous, her permed hair floating in perfect waves about her face, the studio lighting making her skin glow. I looked nothing like this woman either.

"Thank you," I said politely, and waited. Uncle didn't say anything more. He opened the passenger-side door for me and then walked around to the driver's side. And I thought, So this is how it's going to be. We're going to continue to lie to each other.

On the drive into town, Uncle seemed more at ease. He rolled down the windows and let the wind and golden sunshine blow around us.

"So you're a college girl now," he exclaimed. "I'm very proud of you. A good example for your brother and sisters."

"Sam's not going to college. He wants to enlist in the Army," I said. "And the twins want to be Miss Nebraska. They want to run for prom queen. Together."

"There's still time for them. You can become a doctor and show them—"

Suddenly, he was Mister Gung Ho for Education? If he hadn't helped to arrange Sourdi's marriage—at fifteen, while she was still in high school—she might have been able to go to college. Maybe she would've been the doctor. She always liked science more than I did. She liked the fact that she could observe things quietly. I was the noisy one who liked to talk in class all the time.

My heart started racing, the way it'd been doing recently, and I tried to remember what the counselor had said about breathing in through the nose, out through the mouth, calmly, while counting, until I could breathe normally again.

I tried to keep my anger at bay. I hadn't come here for a fight. Not straight away, at least.

Sunlight glinted off the hood of the blue Toyota, and I squinted, shading my eyes with my hand. Palm trees and oleander shrubs rushed by on both sides of the highway.

One hundred, ninety-six, ninety-two, eighty-eight . . .

"Can we listen to the radio?" I asked.

"Certainly. Yes." He turned on the radio, and the dulcet tones of Christian Muzak filled the car.

I closed my eyes to concentrate, sensing a panic attack coming on. Somehow I hadn't imagined that Uncle had become religious.

"Do you mind if we stop at the pâtisserie first? I need to check on business."

"I'm here to help," I said, forcing my voice to sound flat, calm, nothing like I felt inside. I didn't want him to hear the roaring yet. I didn't want the first things I said to him to be embarrassing. "I need to earn some money."

"For school," he said, nodding.

"Yeah."

"Ah," he said, pleased, as though I'd answered a question he hadn't asked aloud. Apparently I'd answered correctly.

Eventually Uncle pulled up to a small donut shop in a strip mall next to a nail salon, a photocopy place, a video rental store, and an Asian grocery with Thai, Khmer, Chinese, and Vietnamese writing on the handmade signs in the window. Uncle's shop had a yellow plastic sign on the red roof with the words "Happy Donuts #3" in large, friendly letters. I recognized Uncle's fussy handwriting on the paper sign that ran the length of the top of the front window: "La Petite Pâtisserie Khmère."

Inside, a tattooed woman of about forty with long auburn hair pulled beneath a hairnet was working behind the counter, boxing chocolate-sprinkled donuts for a woman and her two children. The tattoo on her forearm was a traditional Khmer design to ward off evil, a yantra depicting two tigers and the Sanskrit words for power and authority.

When Sam had spent the summer in Des Moines at a Buddhist temple to gain merit, he had also gained a lot of new friends, boys from cities around the Midwest. Some of them had been in gangs. They had tattoos like this, too.

Sam said it was cool, but Ma wouldn't let him get one.

I wondered why this white American woman had a yantra on her arm.

We waited while she rang up the purchase on a large, old-fashioned cash register, the kind with a cashbox that opened with the clang of a bell. "That'll be five twenty-five, sugar," she told the woman with the kids, and they thanked her and left.

"Hi, Anita," Uncle said. "This is my niece."

"I'm Nea." I held out my hand and waited while Anita wiped her hand on a dishtowel and then shook mine. She had a firm grip. She also had a tattoo of a naga snake with a fanned-out hood arching on the inside of her wrist.

"I've heard so much about you. Your uncle is very proud of you. It's nice to meet you finally," she said. Then she put her hands together in a *sompeah*, the traditional Cambodian greeting, and bobbed her head.

I didn't know what to say. I wondered where she had learned such good manners, but didn't dare ask, as I thought it might seem rude.

"I'm just picking up the next load. I'll take Nea along with me," Uncle told Anita, and they disappeared into the kitchen.

I waited in the front. The shop was less prosperous than I had imagined. There was a single booth, a refrigerated case that held a sparse selection of soda, a Formica counter top that circled in front of the pastry cases, and four swivel stools with cracked, brown vinyl seats. I almost felt sorry for Uncle. He'd never been good at business. I'd somehow assumed that his lack of acumen was due to his constant worries. When Auntie was alive, she was never healthy, always complaining about this or that pain, the side effects of her tranquilizers, about Ma and me. I looked into the empty parking lot, the asphalt colorless under the relentless sunlight. Now I wondered if perhaps running a business was just not his calling.

Anita returned, laughing. She opened one of the pastry cases, pulled out a couple of perfect shell-like madeleines, and popped one into her mouth. "Mmm, mmm. Honey, you've had a long journey, must be feeling a little tired. How about a sugar fix?"

I shook my head, but Anita insisted. "I'm sure there's something to tickle your fancy." She gestured for me to come behind the counter to see the cases up close.

Every kind of pastry I'd ever imagined was crowded along the metal trays: first there were donuts—baked, plain, glazed, powdered, sprinkles, holes (chocolate and glazed), and jelly-filled—then jelly rolls, bear claws dusted with cinnamon and almonds, crisp palmières, éclairs drizzled with dark chocolate and oozing dollops of fresh custard, tiny fruit tarts with glazed berries like fresh kisses preserved in aspic, chocolate-dipped strawberries, crepes in the shapes of small animals, profiteroles made with dough so flaky I could almost taste the butter in the air, croissants, pastel *macarons* in Easter basket shades, and butter cookies drizzled with chocolate, crushed almonds, hardened caramel sauce, dark cocoa, and powdered sugar.

"If you'd come on a Wednesday, we'd have had mousse—strawberry and chocolate." Anita popped a donut hole—chocolate—into her mouth.

"Do you make all these with Uncle?"

"Oh, no, sweetie. Not me. Your uncle's got his groupies." Anita winked at me.

Uncle emerged from the back room, carrying several large cardboard boxes. He set them on the end of the counter, then opened a case and pulled out a long baguette. "You must be hungry, Nea," he said. He sliced it openly neatly, slathered it with butter, and handed it back to me.

I accepted the bread, my stomach suddenly growling. "You know, Uncle, this would be a big hit in a city someplace. Have you ever thought of moving to a better location? Maybe L.A., or Hollywood even?"

"No, no. This is the perfect place for me." Uncle nodded, as though confirming this to himself.

"Oh, they love your uncle here, darling," Anita said.

I looked at the barren parking lot, the customer-less shop, and didn't know what to say.

"Well, time for church," Uncle said. He picked up his boxes.

"It was sure nice to meet you, Nea." Anita waved good-bye.

I followed Uncle out to the parking lot, where he loaded the cardboard boxes into the back seat of the Toyota. I got into the car, trying not to drop baguette crumbs all over the upholstery.

I felt awkward and unhelpful, an intruder. "I'd like to help out, really," I said. "I can start working any time."

Uncle nodded, turned on his religious music channel again, and drove us past strip mall after strip mall until we came up to a small, white, stand-alone building. The sign out front proclaimed, "The Church of Everlasting Sorrow." My heart fluttered uneasily in my chest.

"I want you to meet everyone, Nea," he said happily.

I nodded, a knot in my throat. Ever since I'd been baptized publicly by our sponsors, I'd been wary of the religious. Their aid came with long strings attached, in my experience.

Uncle picked up one of the boxes, and I followed him through the gravel-covered parking lot to the back of the church, where a straggly line of homeless people waited to enter the soup pantry. Uncle rang the bell beside the door, and a tanned priest peered out. He smiled when he saw Uncle.

"Father Juan," Uncle said. "I brought a donation."

The priest slapped Uncle on the back, thanking him and taking the large box. He handed it to a layperson, or a very casually dressed nun, I couldn't tell, and turned back to Uncle. "Your donations are always a big hit around here."

"I want to introduce you to my niece, Nea. She's in college."

"Congratulations," Father Juan said. "Visiting your uncle?"

I nodded. At least he didn't ask me what I was majoring in. *Undeclared* wasn't much of a major.

"We love James," the priest said. "He's one of our most loyal benefactors."

James? I thought.

"No, no," said Uncle modestly. "I just do what I can. Well, we have more donations to make."

"You're welcome to come to Mass any Sunday, you know," Father Juan said.

"I will come someday," he said. "You know I will."

Then I was following Uncle back to his Toyota.

"Was this a special early Christmas donation?" I asked.

Uncle shook his head. "My usual rounds. You'll see. There are so many good people here. They are trying to help many people."

That afternoon we continued making our pastry drops and I met Uncle's grateful beneficiaries: Azaela, who worked at a battered women's shelter; Grace, who volunteered for hospice; Thahn, who ran a youth center; Sophany, who translated at the hospital, and on and on. Everyone thanked him, but no one but me seemed particularly surprised by his generosity. We made several more stops back at the donut shop to pick up more boxes and then spent the rest of the day delivering the boxes until the pastry cases were nearly empty.

"You give it all away?"

"It won't be fresh tomorrow."

"Bag everything up and call it 'Day Old.' Even the grocery stores do that. Put a fake high price on the bag, then write a cheaper price underneath. People will think it's a bargain."

Uncle smiled wanly. "I'll make more tonight."

He'd never been a very good businessman, even when he'd worked with us in the Palace in Nebraska. If it hadn't been for Ma taking over, he'd never have turned a profit. If not for his old buddy Mr. Chhay paying off his loans, Uncle would have lost everything.

I wondered how La Petite Pâtisserie was doing financially.

As the sun was setting and dark shadows were seeping across the parking lot, there was nothing left but donut holes, and, finally, Uncle said it was time to close up. Anita took out the final half dozen and set them on paper doilies. "You have to try these, Nea," she said. "But no peeking."

"But they're all the same," I argued.

"Close your eyes and just taste one. Your Uncle's secret recipe. Tastes different to everyone who tries them. That Mexican priest swears on his Bible they taste like the candy skulls he used to eat growing up, and to some of the bums your uncle feeds at the soup kitchen it tastes like their last home-cooked meal. To the gangbangers who drop by, it's all adrenaline and buzz. They call these things 'crack.'"

"Great," I said. "Like an R-rated version of Willie Wonka."

"Close your eyes," Anita insisted. "Try one and tell me what you taste."

So I obliged.

The dough was soft and chewy, the sugar rough like sand against my tongue. I chewed and chewed, but I couldn't seem to break the donut hole down. It just grew more rubbery, like chewing gum, but without the flavor. I tried to swallow but the mound of dough clung to my teeth. Finally I snatched one of the doilies off the countertop and, turning away, spat out the remains as discreetly as possible.

"Tastes like dust," I gasped, nearly gagging.

"Hmm," Anita looked at me curiously, not as shocked or appalled as I would have imagined. "That's what your uncle always says."

For her part, Anita plucked the remaining donut holes off the counter and popped them into her mouth. "Mmm, mmm," she raved, closing her eyes as she chewed. She swallowed. "Cotton candy, theater popcorn, and a touch of anise."

I was too busy washing the dusty, dry taste away at the fountain, gulping down mouthful after mouthful of water, to answer.

"Shall I stay and help you clean up?" Anita asked Uncle behind me.

"No, it's okay. Take some time off. My niece can help."

"All right, sugar," she said. "I'll see you tomorrow." I turned just in time to see Anita leaning in close to Uncle, and at first I thought she was going to whisper something into his ear, but instead I could have sworn her lips grazed his cheek in a kiss.

Embarrassed, I turned around quickly. I busied myself at the water fountain, pressing the cool metal button and watching the steady stream of water arc back into the basin as though it were the most fascinating thing on earth. I didn't turn even as Anita called out to me, "'Bye, Nea. Sure is nice to meet you!"

The door jangled open and then shut, and I watched Anita walking through the parking lot to her car. The sky was ablaze with pinks and reds, but the temperature was dropping rapidly. I could feel the cold seeping through the glass as the sunlight disappeared. Anita turned once at the end of the parking lot and waved enthusiastically. Composed now, I waved back.

Uncle appeared not to have noticed that I had seen him and Anita. He waved a hand around the room casually. "I can sweep up later when I come back to make the next batch. We should go home now."

I nodded, but before we could leave, a half dozen souped-up cars roared into the parking lot. Engines growled and rap music boomed on the wind. Headlights flashed through the windows.

"Uncle! Uncle!" I heard a young man's voice call out in Khmer.

We're going to get robbed, I thought. I grabbed the phone, ready to call 911.

"It's okay," Uncle said. "I know them."

I watched from the window while Uncle went toward a young man with baggy jeans, a long T-shirt, and tats up and down his arms and encircling his neck like vines trying to pull apart a temple god. The only things that didn't fit with the young man's wannabe thug image were his round, soft Buddha face and the Snugli baby sling dangling from his neck. Uncle said something to him, and the young man nodded, then looked back at the donut shop.

I realized I was standing in the front window, lit up from behind like a display. I tried to duck out of view, but the young man waved at me in an exaggerated manner and gave me a thumbs-up.

I narrowed my eyes at him.

Unintimidated, the thug ran straight up toward the shop. "Hey!" he said, bounding in the front door. "Uncle says you're his niece! You're the one in college!"

"So I guess we're cousins," I said.

He laughed good-naturedly. "Welcome to Magic Donuts," he said. "That's what we call Uncle's dope donuts. They're so good, they're bad."

"They're crack," I said. "I heard."

He laughed again, in a cheerful, good-natured kind of way. The baby in the sling around his neck stirred and began waving its fists in the air. "Uh-oh. The princess is waking up. I better go. I didn't bring her bottle. See you tomorrow, Nea!"

"You're coming back?"

"Oh, yeah. Uncle just hired me." He flashed a white-toothed, horsey smile. "See ya!" Then he ran back outside and rejoined his friends.

I watched from the window as the lowriders bumped their way out of the parking lot.

Uncle came back in. "I'll be ready to go in a minute. I just have to lock up the back." I nodded and waited by the front door.

Now that it was dark, the rest of the strip mall businesses were turning on their Christmas lights, such as they were. A few strings of colored lights across the grocery store window, a flashing outline of a reindeer at the Copy Circle. The employees of the tanning salon plugged a large stand-up Frosty the Snowman into their front window. I watched the red taillights and the white headlights rushing like two candy-cane rivers on the main street in front of the strip mall.

This would be the first Christmas I wouldn't spend with Ma and Sam and the twins since coming to America, and I felt a sudden pang of guilt for lying to Ma. And a little shiver of fear.

I'd either made a very big mistake or I'd made the right decision. It was impossible to know.

CHAPTER 5

The Monk's Cell

Uncle lived in a modest one-bedroom apartment, nothing like the big house he and Auntie had first rented in Nebraska. Back then it seemed like Uncle was still trying to rebuild the life they'd lived before the war, the wealthy life that Auntie missed so much. The new austerity was glaring. The apartment was tidy and spare and mostly empty. I glanced around at the older-model TV with a blinking VCR on a shelf against the wall, the radio on the kitchen countertop, the sofa, the couple of chairs facing the patio that overlooked a palm tree and some geraniums in redwood planters. There were no photographs, but a bookshelf was stacked with paperbacks in four languages: Khmer, French, Chinese, and English. The English ones were mostly self-help, business-type books or genre novels—Westerns and a few mysteries, easy to read, something Uncle might use to improve his English. There was a framed print of Angkor Wat hanging above the bookshelf.

The apartment was spare enough for a monk or some ascetic hermit.

"I hope you're not disappointed. It's not what you're used to. I don't need a big place anymore. It's just me," Uncle said. He pointed to the pile of freshly folded sheets, topped by a towel and washcloth, on the arm of the sofa. "For you. And this folds out. Makes it into a bed."

"Thank you," I said. "This is perfect. Much nicer than my dorm room."

I wasn't lying to be polite. Uncle's big old house had been a nightmare. Too expensive, the bills mounting each month. I used to lie awake in the bed I shared with Sourdi, trying to ignore the sound of Auntie and Uncle's voices traveling through the walls like poltergeists. They'd argued about bills and debts and how noisy we were and whether it had been a good idea to invite us to live with them. Auntie argued it hadn't been.

I realized there was nothing of my birth mother's in this apartment. Uncle must have moved here after Auntie died, I figured, and I felt a shiver of relief run up and down my spine. Then I felt guilty. But mostly I felt relieved.

I set my backpack at the end of the sofa.

"So you should settle in," Uncle said. "My home is your home." He gestured at the kitchenette with the humming Frigidaire in the corner. "There's food. I went to the store this morning."

"I brought gifts from everybody," I said quickly. Which was a lie. I had brought gifts from the university bookstore which I was going to claim were from everyone: Nebraska beef jerky, a paperweight of our mascot, a day planner for the new year.

"No need, no need," Uncle said, smiling distantly. He rubbed the back of his neck with one hand and looked out the window into the streetlights that glowed in the distance like giant irradiated lightning bugs. "I should get back to work."

"But we just left."

"I'm training new bakers. I help them at night. I'm sorry. I will show you around town this weekend."

"Uncle, you work too hard!"

"No, no, it's good," he said. "I like to keep busy. You'll be okay here alone?"

"I'm fine. Can I help you? I'm not tired."

"Not tonight. You should rest. You traveled a long way." He picked up his keys from where he'd placed them on the bookshelf by the door, grabbed a jacket from a hook on the wall, and let himself out.

I sat in the semi-gloom on the edge of the sofa. I had half a mind to get up and take a cab back to the bus station, see how long till the next bus back to Omaha.

I figured I was making Uncle uncomfortable since I was intruding on the new life he'd built for himself. There wasn't a single thing in the apartment that remained of Auntie, or of Ma or of any of us. No family photos, not even the one black-and-white photo from the fancy studio in Phnom Penh that Auntie used to cling to. Nothing.

I didn't know what exactly I'd been hoping for from Uncle, but being left alone in a nearly bare room was not it. Yet he'd told that woman, Anita, that I was coming. She seemed to know who I was. Or at least who I was supposed to be. She'd called me "Nea." She knew I went to college. She said Uncle was proud of me. That thug he'd just hired knew I went to college. So Uncle must have talked about me.

I couldn't figure Uncle out.

I waited another ten minutes, just to make sure Uncle wasn't going to change his mind and come back, and then I jumped up and began investigating the apartment. I searched his bedroom, but it was as spartan as the rest of the apartment. A queen-sized bed with a plain headboard, a few blankets, a dresser with his socks, underwear, and T-shirts folded neatly inside. A few pairs of pants, some shirts, and a couple of blazers hung in his closet.

I wondered if he had a second house somewhere, a place he really lived that he wasn't willing to show me. As I went through his medicine cabinet, I found prescriptions, but nothing exciting. Meds for hypertension, headaches, arthritis. Sudafed. Nicotine gum. Sensitive-gum toothpaste. One toothbrush. A comb with a gray hair winding through the teeth. Tweezers, nail clippers. Something for corns and heavy-duty foot cream. A bottle of Suave two-in-one shampoo and conditioner in the shower, along with a bar of white soap. A towel on the towel bar.

I looked through the trash can under the sink—empty tube of Cankaid, some Kleenex, paper towels used to clean something. I looked through the fridge—a bag of salad greens, Chinese takeout in Styrofoam containers, apples, an orange, soda pop, and a carton of soy milk. The cabinets were almost bare: ramen, rice, Nescafé, tea, bouillon cubes, Campbell's soup, powdered non-dairy creamer, soy sauce, but no fish sauce or even Sriracha. Maybe he had stomach trouble? Maybe he had a secret second family that I didn't know about and he was going to their house? He hadn't told me because he didn't want Ma or Sourdi and Mr. Chhay to find out?

Was he punishing himself for having survived after Auntie died?

I went through the drawers in the kitchen—a cleaver, a couple of butter knives, forks, spoons, a package of disposable chopsticks, a can opener, more Sudafed, matchbooks, emergency candles, a potholder (burned on one edge), plastic wrap, twist ties, sandwich bags, loose rubber bands, a small ball of twine. Under the sink—another garbage can (empty), a box of bargain-brand trash bags, lots of pink plastic bags saved from the Asian grocery store near the donut shop, Comet, Ivory Liquid, a sponge, Mr. Fantastic spray, Lysol, Pinesol, and an unopened bag of sponges. At least he had plenty of cleaning supplies.

I looked in the hall closet by the front door and stood on tiptoe and felt around on the top shelf and pulled down a green plastic bag of Pampers, half-empty. I wondered whose baby needed these diapers.

I wondered if I should look under the mattress, feel if it had been carved out, see if something could be hidden within? Should I use the tool kit and pry open the electric sockets, see if anything was hidden in the walls? All Ma's usual hiding places. But what would be hidden? Uncle's savings? I didn't want money. Our family photo from long, long ago?

Something of Auntie's?

Something of mine?

I sat on the sofa, the light from the ceiling lamp in the kitchen glowing like the reflection of the moon in a puddle, and wondered what I had gotten myself into.

Late that night, I finally unfolded the sofa and made the bed with the sheets Uncle had left folded on the armrest. I wasn't particularly sleepy, but I thought it was the polite thing to do.

I lay in the dark, listening to a mixtape on my Walkman and watching the streetlamps cast shadows of tree limbs and the iron bars of the patio's guardrail across the ceiling.

The air still smelled of sugar and flour, and I realized groggily before I drifted off into a dream that I should have taken a shower while I had the apartment to myself.

I woke to the sound of footsteps. I opened my eyes and saw a shadowy figure standing in the middle of the room. My heart jerked before I realized it was Uncle. He turned, and I closed my eyes quickly, my first reaction, and then waited for him to say something or move or do *something*. But he seemed to be standing still in the middle of the room, doing nothing. Or perhaps he was watching me.

Finally, when I could stand it no longer, I fluttered my eyes open as though I were just awakening from a deep slumber, but the room was empty. No one was standing over me. Uncle was nowhere I could see. I sat up slowly and looked around myself at the dark shapes of the furniture, but I was the only person in the living room. Uncle's bedroom door was closed. I couldn't remember if I'd left it open or not. Quietly, I got up and tiptoed to the door. Leaning close, I listened with my ear cupped to the wood. From deep within, I could hear Uncle's soft snores. He muttered to himself occasionally, an anxious but conversational tone, but I couldn't make out any of the words. He might have been arguing or praying. I couldn't even tell in which language he was dreaming anymore.

CHAPTER 6

The Knife Thrower

The next morning Uncle made us breakfast—omelettes and toast. He must have stopped by the grocery store before coming home last night.

"Just like a hotel," he said grandly, a dish towel draped over his arm as he set my plate before me. "Voilà, Mademoiselle." I giggled despite myself at his fancy manners.

He sat across from me at the table and picked up his fork and knife. "So, do you like your university? You are the first member of our family in America to go to school."

"It's okay," I said.

He nodded. "What is your major?"

"I'm still undeclared." I tried to think of a way to change the subject. "The donut shop is a lot of work for you."

"I know that university is very expensive in America. I will help you out, of course."

So that's why he thinks I'm here? To make him pay for my college? I put my fork down. If he wanted to play games, I might as well forget about being polite and just confront him. Ask him why he didn't tell me that he was really my father, not my uncle. I took a deep breath, and the dry, burnt feeling of toast crumbs coated the back of my throat. I coughed and coughed.

Alarmed, Uncle poured a glass of water and offered it to me.

Tears welled up in my eyes, and I took huge gasps of air, like a fish that had leaped too high and accidentally beached itself onto its river's bank. I struggled not to panic. Finally, when I could stop coughing, I drank the glass of water, but my throat still felt as though it were coated in fiberglass.

"Don't worry. We shouldn't talk of important things when we're eating," Uncle said. He took my plate.

I gulped more water. "Sorry."

Uncle shook his head. "If you're ready, we can go."

And so we headed back to the donut shop without my getting any closer to the truth.

Anita was already at work. She was serving up donuts for a line of nurses in scrubs who were either on their way to work or possibly on their way home after a night shift.

Miraculously, all the cases were filled with new pastries.

The air smelled like sugar and coffee, with just a faint whiff of Anita's cigarette smoke.

Then I saw him behind the counter, the thug from last night. He was wearing a white apron over a white T-shirt and torn jeans, and his muscled arms were covered in tattoos: long lines of Khmer script, four Chinese characters, and a snarling tiger. I almost didn't notice that his right hand was injured. His thumb and index finger were missing.

"Hi there, sugar," Anita called out. "Have a bite before you get to work."

"Thanks, but we already ate," I said, and I followed Uncle into the kitchen. There were giant batter-spattered metal bowls, rotary blades, spatulas, and baking trays piled high in the stainless steel sinks. "You must have an army of people come in overnight." I whistled. "I can start on the dishes."

"Sitan will help you. Normally he'll be back here, but it's busy this morning." Uncle disappeared into a supply closet and re-emerged with a pile of flattened cardboard boxes.

"More donations?" I asked.

Uncle nodded. "I'll be back soon. Just have to make my morning rounds."

I knew he was going to give away half his stock again, and the businesswoman in me cringed. But I wasn't here to tell Uncle how to run his business. I bit my tongue.

"You want me to help you assemble all those?"

Uncle looked distracted, and, for a second, he seemed not to understand what I'd said to him. He looked at me sadly, then looked back at the pile of cardboard.

"It's no problem," I said, and gently took one of the boxes from him and folded it along its scored sides. "I can do them all."

"I never thought—" Uncle began, then stopped. He turned away.

"Are you all right?" I wondered if he might actually be ill. He seemed paler, and he was blinking rapidly.

"I'm very happy you're here," Uncle said, but he wouldn't look at me.

After I folded up all the boxes, Uncle filled them with fresh pastries and headed out. Neither Anita nor Sitan seemed surprised by his behavior.

The morning rush had petered out and there was only a young mother with a toddler on her hip grabbing a morning donut.

The thug flirted with her shamelessly, and the woman blushed and smiled and ordered an extra bear claw to go.

"He's a charmer, isn't he?" Anita nudged me. "All the ladies fall in love with him."

I rolled my eyes. "Not my type," I said.

The mother with the toddler headed out, glancing one last time over her shoulder as she waved with her fingertips. I refrained from groaning.

There was a loud cry from a baby seat parked in the corner booth, and at first I thought the woman had actually been so distracted that she'd left her kid behind. Then Sitan hopped over the counter and rushed to the baby's side, cooing and rattling a toy at it.

"You brought your kid?"

"Daycare's a waste of money. What's it to you?"

"Now, you two, don't fight. I have something to show you. You'll never guess what I found waiting for me when I got home last night." Anita hurried into the kitchen through the swinging doors and returned with a compact box. She hefted it onto the countertop. "My knives came," she said proudly.

"Yo, that's dope," Sitan proclaimed.

"Now where did James put the scissors?" She searched through the drawers behind the counter.

Sitan pulled out a Swiss Army knife attached to his jeans by a chain. Holding the package steady with the three fingers on his right hand, he held the knife with his left and carefully sliced open the packing tape.

Anita sorted through the Styrofoam peanuts and pulled out a large knife attached by several dozen twist ties to a thick square of cardboard.

"Is that like a Ginsu?" I squinted at the writing on the package.

"It slices, it dices. It can cut a can, it can slice a tomato! But wait! There's more!" Sitan put on his best infomercial voice.

"No, these are even better," Anita said. She patiently, carefully untwisted the ties, one by one. "These are my throwing knives."

"Anita used to be famous," Sitan said. "She was on *That's Incredible!*, magicians of the world episode." Sitan added, proudly, "I saw it."

"You're too young."

"No, I swear, I saw it. You were da bomb, Anita." He smiled so that all his strong, white teeth showed. I could see how some women might find him attractive.

"You were a magician? That's amazing," I said to Anita.

Anita narrowed her green eyes a little, just enough for me to imagine what she might look like when she was genuinely angry. "Oh, honey, no. I don't do *illusions*." She reacted as though I'd accused her of turning tricks. "I'm a knife thrower. I filled in between acts while the magicians were setting up backstage."

"She can throw flaming spears, too."

"Among other things. But mostly I specialized in knives," Anita said. She took out the long, pointed knife and held it up to the light as she examined the blade.

"That actually looks really sharp," I said. "I always thought those knives were fake in those shows. So nobody would get hurt."

Anita and Sitan turned to each other in disbelief and laughed. Sitan bounced his baby on his hip. "You hear that, Lillian? College Girl thinks they're fake!" He made his eyes bulge out comically, and his daughter giggled, too.

Anita shook her head. "Don't touch my knives, sugar. They're sharp all right." She pulled a paper napkin out of the metal dispenser on the counter and held it over her knife blade, then let the napkin fall. The paper fell into two shivering halves as it hit the metal edge.

"Show her what it'll do to a Coke can, Anita!" Sitan ran over to the cooler case and pulled out a Coca-Cola. "Here."

"No, no, no. I don't want to waste the blade. But if you're interested—"

"Yeah! Do it, Anita! Show her!"

"I can throw a few for you."

"You mean, like at a target?" Not at a human target, I hoped.

She smiled girlishly and turned to wink at Sitan. She pulled off her apron and folded it neatly on the countertop. "Well then. Let's go out back, Nea."

I followed Anita out the kitchen door, where there was a dumpster and a pile of scrap wood and broken cinder blocks. Anita set one of the wood boards on the blocks, which she kicked into place with her foot. She took a step back, squinted, then nodded.

"That should do it," she said. "Come here. I'll show you something."

Anita set the knife case on the asphalt beside her and opened it with a click. The sunlight glinted off the long, thin blades within. She pulled her hair back with a scrunchie. Then she slowly raised her right hand and peered between the V formed by her index and middle fingers, while she picked up a knife with her left hand. There was a loud THWONK! The knife hit the board point-first and remained lodged there.

"Five inches to the right." Anita picked another knife up and, again, it hit the board with a THWONK! before I even knew she'd released it.

"Call it," Anita said.

"Um, three inches from the bottom."

Anita smiled and winked at me, then peered through her fingers, and, once again, hit her mark.

"Damn, you are good!" I said. "Why'd you stop?"

"Ah, I killed a person." Anita waited a beat, then laughed. "Just kidding. Carpal tunnel syndrome. That and tennis elbow. And golf shoulder. Plus I herniated a disc in my neck. But it's not the injuries. To be honest, I got lonely. Too much traveling, too many hotel rooms. I didn't get to watch my kids grow up, and then, seems before I knew it, they were married with kids of their own. My marriages never lasted." Anita shrugged and retrieved her knives from the board, pulling each one out with a sharp flick of her wrist.

"Anita used to throw in Bangkok. She was in Phnom Penh, too," Sitan said. "That's where she got her dope tat."

"And Battambang and Sihanoukville. I only regret I never made it to Saigon. Those were the days. U.S. government was sponsoring all kinds of wholesome entertainment in the region, trying to keep the people on the so-called good side. I got to travel all over Southeast Asia. There was this one couple from Hong Kong, wife was some kind of movie star. I remember she used to do a little song-and-dance number. It was supposed to promote positive feelings. Soft power, they call it."

"You're kidding me. Was this for the military?"

"I'm a pacifist. I don't do military shows." Anita shook her head. "Not like some of the magic acts I could name. They'd perform for anybody who paid. No scruples whatsoever. But that's what I'd expect from an illusionist." She packed her knives back into their case lovingly.

"Is that how you met my uncle? In Cambodia?" I had to ask.

"Oh, no, no, no. I wish I'd known him then. We met at the hospital here. I was going in for my carpal tunnel syndrome and he was volunteering, translating for some of the refugee families. One thing led to another, and he hired me to work for him at the pâtisserie."

Something about the tone of her voice, the way it changed just slightly, and the flush in her cheeks, the flutter of her lashes, made it sound as though she were talking about the start of a love affair and not a job at a donut shop.

Anita locked up her case. Her tone turned brisk, "We should head back in. Never know when a customer might pop over."

Sitan followed Anita into the shop, begging her to teach him how to throw knives, too.

"You weren't born a lefty. I don't know if you'd have the coordination, and I don't want to be responsible if something awful happens."

I let them go on ahead. I hung back and took the makeshift target off the cinderblock base, fingering the holes in the plywood made by the knives.

Suddenly, I had more sympathy for my birth mother. Even if Uncle hadn't met Anita yet, there would have been other women, and Auntie was so jealous. To know she'd lost her beauty, her children, her standing, and see her husband whole, attractive to other women. That kind of bitterness could kill somebody. Maybe it had killed her.

A little before noon it started getting busy again, but amidst the lines of customers I recognized the young men from last night. They pulled up in a red Maserati lowrider with rims and new whitewalls. Music loud enough to hear inside the donut shop despite our boom box playing the Earth, Wind & Fire mixtape Anita favored.

Sitan looked up from the cash register.

"Gotta go, Anita," he said, pulling his apron off his head. "Gotta practice. Can you cover for me?"

"Practice what?" I asked. "Skipping out on work?"

"You go on, Sitan, honey. I've got your back." Anita winked at him. "But you better remember me when you're rich and famous."

Sitan's soft Buddha face melted into a smile. "I'm buying you a mansion, Anita. You better check out the real estate in Beverly Hills. The nine-oh-two-one-oh, just for you."

Sitan grabbed the baby seat where his daughter slept and practically skipped out the front door, brushing past customers.

He slapped the hands of his friends, then jumped into the Maserati and roared out of the parking lot.

"They're not going to rob a bank or something," I sneered to Anita as she rung up an order of crullers.

"He's going to be a big rap star someday," Anita said.

"Oh, brother."

"He's very talented. I've heard him."

"Glad he's got a backup plan in case the donuts don't work out for him," I said.

Anita gave me a glinty-eyed stare. "Everybody has to have a dream. Not everybody gets to go to college."

I felt embarrassed then. I didn't know when I'd become such a snob.

Shortly after two, business had slowed. Actually it stopped completely, and I went over to a stir-fry place down the street and bought lunch for Anita and me. We were sitting in the booth, eating our noodles and Buddha's delight, talking about Anita's "show business days," as she called them, and sharing a cigarette, when Uncle returned.

He must've parked in the back and come in the kitchen without our hearing. I was facing the counter, my back to the wall in the corner booth, when Uncle popped into the donut shop. He was hurrying in the front door, his thoughts else-where and a slightly distracted look on his face, when he saw me. He blanched, as though he'd seen a ghost. He stood stock still for a second, frozen, then scurried back into the kitchen without speaking a word to either of us.

I'd seen his expression as he looked at me, first blank, like "Who is that?" and then the shock, the way his features jumped, when he remembered. He looked like he'd seen the dead.

"What's up, Hon'?" Anita asked. Her back was to the door, and she hadn't even noticed Uncle coming in.

"Uncle's back."

She craned her neck, looking around, before she realized he'd disappeared without saying hello. Then she turned back to me, a fake smile plastered on her face, and I could immediately tell why Anita hadn't succeeded on the knife-throwing circuit. She couldn't fake a smile. She looked at me now with anxious, sad eyes and her lips pulled back from her teeth. I imagined that a wild animal trying to bluff a bigger opponent in a fight at a watering hole might look like this just before it got eaten.

My nose burned, and then my eyes started to water, and I knew I was feeling sorry for myself. I hated myself even more. I picked up my Styrofoam takeout container and threw it in the trash. The smell of sugar was oppressive. I couldn't swallow properly. My throat felt as though it were narrowing.

"I'm going for a walk," I managed to rasp to Anita, and I stumbled out the door without waiting for her reply.

The sunlight was too bright. The asphalt was bleached white, sticky under my sneakers. I squinted and tried to keep moving, one foot in front of the other, but the world felt as though it were tilting. In my memories I was being rejected all over again. I was eight years old, walking onto the playground in Texas for the first time, and the girls circled Sourdi and me, pulling the skin back from their eyes, taunting us, and I had no idea what I'd done wrong. I was eleven, meeting Auntie for the first time in Nebraska, and she looked at me as though inspecting for damage, my every gesture an insult, my voice too loud, my accent too American, my ways too bold. Everything that had been good about me became wrong all over again.

Now the world was spinning and the sky turned white and then black, like a photo negative. I sat down on the curb in front of the Asian grocery. I could smell the fresh bok choy wilting in the heat of the afternoon sun, overripe mangoes, cilantro, and a dusty scent from the root-vegetable bins. My head felt very heavy and fell against my knees. I held it in place with both hands.

I was wrong to come here. Uncle hated me. He was only pretending he'd been happy to see me. I was wrong. I made him unhappy. When Auntie was alive, I'd made her unhappy too, when I was just a kid.

When she ran the Palace with Ma, Auntie had nothing but complaints about me. I clomped when I walked, I shouted when I spoke, I showed all my teeth when I smiled. I was too tall, I ate too much. I wasn't dainty. Auntie saw me get in a fight in the parking lot. Three white boys attacked my sisters and brother and me during our first week in Nebraska. I fought them off. I saved the rocks they threw at us and threw them back, and, terrified, they fled on their bikes. I thought it was a victory, but Auntie saw it all from the window in the Palace and thought it was shameful.

She didn't care that I'd saved my siblings. She didn't care that the boys threw the rocks at us first. She didn't care that no one else had come to help us when I'd screamed. She didn't like me. I was a disappointment.

I didn't know then that she was my mother.

She missed her oldest son. But finding me alive had been a disappointment.

I was no reason for her to try to stay alive.

I was everything wrong that could have happened to her daughter.

Maybe she wished she'd never found me. Maybe she wished I had died.

Maybe Uncle wished that now.

I could taste the fried noodles on the back of my tongue. The grease, the salt, the soy sauce and MSG. I breathed through my mouth, trying not to be ill.

I didn't want to throw up in public, where people could see, strangers, the girls who worked in the grocery, the men who worked in the video store, the who-knows-who potential customers in the parking lot.

Something cold and wet nudged the side of my arm, and I jumped.

One of the checkers from the grocery was holding a cold can of 7Up in her hand. "You okay?"

I nodded.

"Take it. Don't work too hard," she said with a smile, and went back inside.

I mouthed, "Thanks," as though she could still see me, and opened the soda. The pop! and hiss, so familiar, made me feel better. Sometimes the smallest acts of kindness made me melt.

I took a sip of the soda. It was too sweet against my teeth, but it was like the treasured cans of pop we used to share when I was a kid. When we first came to America, the Church Ladies never gave us soda pop in the bags of groceries they brought. And food stamps didn't let us get brand names either. If Ma bought us a soda, we had to share it. I didn't even like the taste at first, but I'd seen kids on TV drinking Coca-Cola and Pepsi and 7Up, smiling and strong and running and popular and happy, and I wanted to be just like them. I wanted to give the world a Coke, too. I wanted to take the Pepsi Challenge. I liked the pretty green cans of Sprite with the fancy lettering I couldn't read yet, not like the ugly type on the generic soda we could afford.

We used to blindfold ourselves, using an undershirt that Sourdi tied around our heads, take sips from the same can of soda, and say, "It's Coke!" or "It's Pepsi!" Sourdi would make a buzzer sound or a "ding!" like a bell, depending on her mood, to signal if we were correct or wrong.

Then Sam would exclaim, "I can't believe I like Pepsi better!" and slap his forehead just like the man in the commercial, and we'd laugh and laugh.

Sitting on the curb in front of the grocery, facing the donut shop, I drank the whole can of 7Up that the girl had given me. It still tasted like a luxury.

Then I went back to work.

Nobody was working in the donut shop when I returned. I peeked into the kitchen and spotted Anita and Uncle conferring by the mixers. I was going to tell them that I was back and that I'd man the register, but something about the furtive way they huddled together made me hesitant to interrupt.

"I haven't seen you look this down in a while," Anita was saying. "Is it Nea?"

My heart stopped. Then started up with a jerk.

"She looks just like Sopheam . . . When they were the same age," Uncle's voice sounded strangled, stretched too taut. "I see her and I remember everything."

"Does she know?"

"We don't talk about these things."

Then the bell on the door rang behind me, like a really big cat bell signaling the arrival of a customer, and I quickly shut the swinging door to the kitchen and jumped behind the counter, hoping Uncle and Anita hadn't realized I'd been spying on them, and wouldn't know that I'd heard them and that I knew Uncle was sorry I'd come.

PART THREE

You do not fear the thorny plant (underfoot), yet you fear the tiger (far away).

—traditional Cambodian proverb

CHAPTER 7

The Sisters Who Turned into Birds

Ma used to tell me a folktale, the story of the three sisters who turned into birds. We must have been living in the refugee camp, where it was safe to tell stories again. Under the Khmer Rouge, stories were forbidden, language was dangerous, and we had to be quiet all the time. I loved Ma's stories, but I was hungry, I kept interrupting, I didn't let her finish.

Once there were three little girls who were living alone with their widowed mother when she remarried to a wealthy gangster from the city.

"What kind of food do they eat for the wedding?" I asked.

"Hush now, noisy girl, or I won't finish the story."

"But he's a gangster. They must have a lot of food." There were gangsters in the refugee camp, men who controlled bands of boys who roamed the tents looking for things to steal—clothing and jewelry, knives and machetes, coconuts and the shells of nuts, small lizards that could be eaten, and once a hand grenade with a broken pin. The gangsters were scary and could steal your food if they caught you alone, if you were small, if you showed fear. "Please, tell me. Please, please, tell me what they ate."

Finally Ma sighed and rolled onto her back, folding her hands over her flat stomach.

"Chicken curry and ginger-shred chicken and beef noodle soup and cellophane noodles with tiny shrimp on top. Three bowls each of steamed white rice. Everyone eats an entire mango each."

Satisfied, I licked my lips and let her continue the story.

The mother begins to dress and act like a rich woman. She neglects the animals and leaves the chores to her children. She spends all her time in the city with the gangster, wearing fancy clothing, eating fancy food, talking and drinking with the gangster's friends. She acts as though she has no children at all. When she comes home, she sees her three daughters waiting in the doorway, calling out to her for food. She decides to get rid of them once and for all. The next day she takes them into the jungle and leaves them there. She sprinkles rice in a looping circle so the beasts of the jungle will be sure to find them in the center. Then she goes home and leaves them to their fate.

Lying next to Ma under the mosquito net, I knew how the little girls must have felt as they huddled together in the dark that fell all at once like a curtain, so that the sun suddenly disappeared in the jungle and only the absence of light remained. The girls could hear the cries of the hungry animals rising to hunt. Panther cries, tiger growls. The leaves rustled with snakes. The air buzzed with bats. Something high-pitched shrieked. The sisters held each other and sobbed.

I knew because I remembered what it had been like when we had to walk through the jungle to escape. When we fled the village controlled by the soldiers and walked at night together, Ma and Sourdi, Sam and the twins, all of us were quiet—quiet like mice, like rabbits, like small vulnerable creatures—while the jungle roared around us.

"Don't worry," Ma said. "Don't cry. It's just a story."

"I know," I said, wiping my eyes on the back of my hand. "What happened next?"

The spirit of the forest hears the little girls crying in the dark and takes pity. It isn't right, it's against the natural order of the world, little girls alone amongst beasts. The spirit sends the wind to confuse the wild animals, disguising the sweet fleshy scent of the girls with jasmine and poison oleander, with stinkweed and durian, with rotting moss and fetid marsh.

The next morning, shafts of sunlight fall through the canopy of leaves like golden swords. The sisters rub their eyes and see the rice their mother has strewn about the jungle floor, glowing white as pearls. They eat the rice and follow the trail home.

When their mother sees the girls emerge from the jungle, calling her name and running toward her, she is filled with a liquid rage that sloshes against the backs of her eyes. She picks up a hoe and chases them back into the jungle. Terrified, the girls run and run and run until they are completely lost.

The spirit of the forest does not know what to do with three little human girls. At first the spirit simply tricks the animals to keep them away, but the girls grow hungry and cry. They grow thinner and thinner, their bones threatening to pierce their skin. The spirit tries to leave them food: meat fresh from a tiger's conquest, seeds still in their pods, mushrooms and fungus and berries, raw things the beasts of the jungle might eat themselves. At first the girls are unwilling to eat such things, but then one day they fall upon the spirit's food, eating ravenously. Day after day they eat like wild creatures until it is too late. Their lips grow hard and pointed, more like beaks than mouths. Little feathers sprout on their chests, their arms turn into wings, the pinion feathers long and graceful. Their bodies shrink, and the last tatters of their human clothes fall to the jungle floor. The girls stare at each other in amazement, but when they open their mouths, no words come out. The wind swirls about them, scattering their meal of seeds and berries and flesh, and the girls run into the spirit wind and fly away, high high high above the trees.

"What could they see?" I wanted to know. "Could they see their mother? Their house?"

"No." Ma was growing tired. Her breath had slowed. I could feel her body growing heavier, like a stone beside me. I could feel her leaving me, drifting to another realm.

I pinched her arm. I scratched her calf with the sharp broken nail of my big toe. "Did they fly to their mother's house?"

"Mmm. No."

"Why not?" Frantically, I pulled on my mother's shirt, I breathed on her face, blew across her nose, hoping my hot breath would wake her. "Why didn't they fly to see their mother?"

Ma stirred. "They didn't want to see her."

"Not even to see what she was doing?"

"They didn't remember her. They were birds now."

"Oh."

The people of the village are watching the mother behaving like a gangster herself. They shake their heads. They know what she's done to her daughters. What kind of mother is she? Not a good woman. Not someone they wanted in their village.

So the villagers band together and drive the mother and the gangster out of the village. They then tear down her house and burn the wood. They take all the woman's animals; they steal all the woman's pots and pans and bowls and cups. They take her sarong and her krama scarf and the comb she used in her hair. They pretend the woman never lived there at all.

(I nod. This is exactly what villagers would do.)

After many years, the girls' father returns to the village.

"He wasn't really dead?" I gripped Ma's arm tightly in my excitement.

"Sshh. Quiet."

"But I thought the mother was a widow?"

"No. She just thought her husband was dead." Ma was growing sleepy. Her voice was heavy, slow, the way we used to move under the sun, turning the earth slowly with our borrowed hoes.

I nudged her gently, then not so gently. "So the father returns?" I prompted.

Ma blinked, licked her lips, and reached into the dark for my hand. Finding it in hers, she squeezed it tight and continued.

So the father returns and discovers the scorched spot where his house once stood. He asks the villagers, "Where is my wife? Where are my children?" But they pretend they don't know. Alarmed, he walks to the city. He asks in the market if anyone has seen his wife, a woman this high, with three girls trailing behind? People shake their heads and turn away. Stall after stall, no one will speak. Finally an old woman takes pity and tells him the story of his dissolute wife marrying the gangster and the way she'd taken the children to the forest to die.

The father marches into the forest himself, carrying a pack upon his back, a long knife in one hand to fight the beasts, and a long stick in the other to help him walk through the pathless jungle, over the tall grasses and the thick vines and the dark low-lying branches.

The bird sisters see their father walking through the forest. They call out to him, but they can no longer remember how to speak. Their beaks open and shut, open and shut, but they can only cry in birds' voices. The father looks up and sees his children circling above his head, shrieking, but he does not recognize them. They have turned completely into birds.

Ma drifted away from me into her dreamless sleep. I held on to her hand all night, thinking about the bird girls, flying freely above the jungle, the sunlight strong against their feathers, the wind carrying them higher and higher, the beasts below them small as insects. Could they see the villages where we toiled? Could they see the soldiers with their guns walking two by two so no one can escape? Could they see all the way to the ocean? I imagined the bright blue water stretching to the long curved edge of the world, like the map that hangs on the plywood wall of the makeshift classroom in the refugee camp. The one the teacher points to when she shows us where the lucky families go when they are sponsored to leave. I was thrilled by the idea that I, too, might turn into a bird. Such lucky girls, I thought.

I never thought to wonder: Did they ever miss their human parents? Did they miss their mother even though she'd sent them away? Did she ever tell them stories? Did they ever wonder why she changed?

Nor did I think much about their father, who could not recognize their cries. How long did they cry out to him? How long before they gave up and flew away?

This was how my nights passed in the refugee camp.

CHAPTER 8

The Plan

That night as I lay on the sofa, I tried to think of what I could offer Uncle. Right now I was taking up space, eating his food, earning no money. No wonder I felt like a burden.

Before I gave up and went back home, back to college, I had to try harder. I couldn't give up after a couple of days. I was sure there was a way to win Uncle over. To show him that I was a good daughter, one he'd be willing to acknowledge, one he'd be proud to call his own. I wasn't just someone who reminded him of all that was unhappy about the past, of the wars and all that had been lost.

I needed to show him I could be useful.

Uncle loved the donut shop. He spent all his time there. He'd even given it a special fancy name. If I could make it into a success, I figured, he'd be happy to have me around.

I got up from the couch and pulled the Yellow Pages out from under the phone. I took out my notebook and pencil from my backpack and began to list our competition, trying to see if we had any advantage in terms of location, bus routes, price, service, anything. I knew we could beat anyone on flavor, but how to let people know?

I brainstormed a list of promotions: manning tables in front of grocery stores or bus stops like kids selling Girl Scout cookies. Give-aways at beauty parlors, nail shops, tanning salons, video stores, and florists, all these little businesses in the endless strip malls. Maybe I should pack up a variety box and donate them to the cops? Thank them for their service to the community, write up a card, and drop a box by? I didn't trust cops myself—when had they ever helped my family?—but they might be useful to have around, keep the gangs away. And, rumor had it, they like donuts.

By the time the light seeping through the crack in the curtains was the bluish color of skim milk, I had a list of promotions two pages long. I was dozing off when I heard the newspaper thwack against the apartment door.

I checked my watch. It was twenty after five and Uncle still hadn't come home.

Rubbing my face with one hand, I staggered to the door to get the paper, a thin local called the *Santa Bonita Times*. There was a picture of a girl in pigtails holding a bunny under the headline: "Local Girl's Prize Rabbit Returned." Some kid's pet went missing for five weeks and then showed up again mysteriously on her family's doorstep accompanied by an album of photographs showing the bunny in front of famous places: the Hollywood sign, Universal Studios, the beach, the Golden Gate Bridge, Muir Woods, and the Hearst Castle. Some people had too much time on their hands, I decided. The other news was typical small-town fare: there'd been a fire in an apartment complex, a rash of break-ins in a trailer park, a fight (non-fatal) at a nightclub, a flower show sponsored by the Junior League, a middle-school play, and a preview of the upcoming Parade of Homes featuring a series of photos of houses dripping with Christmas decorations (obnoxious). AP wire stories covered a roundup of world and national news. The last pages were devoted to sports and comics. They didn't even have *Bloom County* or *The Far Side*, just old-timey stuff like *Family Circle* and *Brenda Starr*.

All this and they led with the bunny, I thought.

I looked for the masthead and the names of the editors. A paper like this might like a feature on a new Grand Opening. I could see La Petite Pâtisserie Khmère bumping the bunny from its place of honor above the fold. Uncle and me standing side by side and smiling in front of the pastry case, or, better yet, holding out a tray of fresh donuts enticingly.

I'd show him what I could do.

And maybe, I thought, there could be a follow-up article: "Father and Daughter, Separated by War, Reunite in Santa Bonita." Surely we were a bigger story than the bunny. It would be a full page, with photographs. I could put the clipping in an album, show it to my roommate in college. Flip the page open casually as Shannon showed off her ski trips to Vail, her camping trips in the Rockies. "Oh, while I was on my personal leave, I reunited with my father. We'd been separated by the Khmer Rouge, but now we've found each other." Show my dormmates the smiling photos. They'd be shocked. What an amazing story! I wouldn't tell them that I'd known my father earlier and he'd pretended to be my uncle. I'd say instead, He didn't recognize me before. I'd say, He was so happy to learn I was still alive.

Maybe the local TV news would pick it up and then we'd go national. We might make it on *The Today Show*, or even *Oprah*.

I could picture myself sitting on her sofa next to Uncle, who now explained that he'd had amnesia, a kind of PTSD that the doctors didn't know about. He'd describe the moment when he finally recognized me, the feeling in his chest of his heart opening up, the weights like heavy stones lifting, how he felt as light as air, as though he could dance hovering six inches above the ground. I would smile modestly while the studio audience sighed and tears welled up in Oprah's eyes. I would buy a new dress just for the show. I tried to imagine the color—red for our love, yellow like the sun for our happiness, blue to match my hair.

Then the front door to the apartment opened and Sitan staggered in.

I jumped up.

"Oh, hey. Uncle gave me the—um, you know, whatcha call-em." He tossed the keys on the top of the bookshelf.

"Are you drunk?"

"Chill, girl. Been out with my homeboys." He tried to take off his shoes and fell over. He lay back on the carpet, his hands on his stomach.

"Aren't you working in the shop now?"

"Mmm hmm." He was drifting off to sleep.

Disgusted, I gathered up my clothes and locked myself in the bathroom to get dressed. When I came out, Sitan was snoring loudly on the floor.

The phone rang, startling me.

I ran to the kitchen. "Hello?"

It was Uncle. "Nea, is Sitan there?"

"Just arrived. He passed out on the floor."

"Thank goodness. I wanted to make sure he got home safely."

"He's not home," I pointed out. "He's on the floor of *your* apartment."

"He must be very tired." Uncle sounded worried. "Just let him sleep. He can come in later when he wakes up again."

"I don't think I could wake him if I tried. His royal highness seems pretty plastered."

Uncle sighed. "He's been doing so well. He's been making a lot of progress."

I decided not to argue. "I won't wake him up. Are you coming back now?"

"No, I can't. I'm sorry. There was a call. A family needs a translator. I'm going to the hospital to help. Don't worry. You can just stay at home today."

"Uncle, you've worked all night. You should rest."

"I'm fine." He hung up.

And I thought, he's going to drop dead if he keeps working like this. Then a worse thought came to me. Maybe Uncle was *trying* to work himself to death. Maybe this was how his survivor's guilt was manifesting. Like a death wish. And what would Ma say if I just stood by and let that happen?

I paced in the kitchenette as the cheerful yellow light from the rising sun began to pour inside, lapping at the countertops and the white Frigidaire, splashing against the walls like a wave of honey. I peered out the window into the parking lot, and watched sparrows wheel across the sky, which grew brighter and more blue with each passing minute. A hummingbird hovered by the bougainvillea. It was hard to remember that it was December, that Christmas was only two weeks away. I'd left Nebraska fallow and frozen and taken a bus to arrive in a whole other season. Traffic zoomed by on the street below, and I watched as a bus barreled past; an ad for *Die Hard 2* wrapped around the bus featuring a Christmas wreath superimposed over Bruce Willis's shoulders.

Something about the combination of December and blooming flowers and warm sunshine made me feel unnaturally optimistic. I flipped open the phone book on the kitchen table and examined the map of bus routes in the front so that I could head to the donut shop on my own. Better to get working on my PR plan than to wait in the apartment listening to Sitan snore.

Anita was surprised to see me when I came running in the front door. "I took the bus," I announced proudly.

"It's been kind of a slow morning. But I'm happy to have your company." She looked up from the paper, where she'd been working on the crossword. "Would you like coffee or are you a Coca-Cola in the morning type of girl?"

"Coffee, thanks." I pulled my notebook out of my backpack. "You know, I was thinking of ways to drum up more business. The pastry is fantastic. People just don't know this place is here. It doesn't look special."

"Your uncle's kind of low-key about the business end," Anita said. "He got a small-business grant to train people. I helped him write up the proposal myself. I think he thinks of himself more as an educator than a businessman."

"Well, I think of myself more as a capitalist," I said. Then I showed her my list of marketing ideas. "I thought I could make some of these flyers over at the copy shop. What do you think? I want to help Uncle. I want him to be happy. I don't want to be a burden. I want to show him I can earn my keep."

"You're not a burden, Nea," Anita said. "James is very proud of you. You have no idea. He's told me so much about you."

"That's a surprise."

"He doesn't always say what he's thinking or feeling. That's not his way."

"I haven't done anything yet," I said, growing impatient. I threw three creamers into the coffee and gulped it down. "Since it's slow, I'm going over to the Copy Circle right now and I'll get started. Just give me a call over there if it gets busy and you need help."

"Take your time, Nea," Anita said. She looked down at the counter and pursed her lips as though she wanted to say something more, but then thought better of it. "You should do what you think is right, of course."

"Great," I said. "See you later!"

And I ran out the door and across the parking lot, confident I could make a difference.

I typed up coupon offers, flyers, and finally the letter to the reporter from the newspaper who'd had the front-page story about the runaway rabbit. I told him I had an even better story for him. I told him about all of Uncle's travails—having to flee Cambodia shortly before the Khmer Rouge took over in 1975, living as a refugee, coming to America. "The chaos of war caused Mr. Chhouen Suoheang to flee his own country. He hoped to send for his family after he'd settled in a safe country, but alas the Khmer Rouge sealed the borders and he was separated from them for years. Two of his sons died under Pol Pot. He was reunited with his wife in the United States. Unfortunately she was ill after sustaining injuries during her escape through a minefield and died in California." I thought it best to leave out the complicated parts, the troubled reunion, the poverty, the illnesses, the fighting, Auntie's overdose. And me, the forgotten daughter. These were the details that I'd witnessed, that I'd lived through, but they weren't going to get Uncle any customers, I figured. Papers that led with stories about cute bunnies liked a softer version of life. So I cut to the chase: "Out of this tragedy, he has now opened La Petite Pâtisserie Khmère to train former refugees. He believes in giving back to the community that has offered him safe harbor after so much tragedy. The Petite Pâtisserie Khmère serves the best French-Cambodian pastry in Southern California."

I put down the address and phone number. Then I bought a stamp and mailed the letter right away.

For the next three days, I busied myself placing flyers in the strip malls up and down the street and in the foyers of the apartment compounds in the neighborhood. I accompanied Uncle on his volunteer rounds and left flyers with coupons at the hospital and the youth center. We needed to get these people to come into the shop on their own. They were spoiled. But with any luck, they could develop a sugar habit, and, most importantly, come pay for our donuts rather than waiting for them to be delivered free.

For three days, I put on my happiest face. I didn't argue, I didn't complain. Uncle seemed to relax around me finally. Or perhaps it was because Sitan stayed over at the apartment for two of those days, and Uncle liked having him around. He liked to give him advice and ask how many bookings he'd gotten for rapping at local clubs, and when Sitan said he didn't have any at present but this owner he knew liked him and was going to give him a chance in the new year, they just had to work out the details, Uncle clapped his hands together and nodded, "You see! All your hard work is paying off." And because I was being good and pleasant, I refrained from rolling my eyes and instead said, "That's great, Sitan. Congratulations."

But despite my efforts, Sitan merely flashed me an angry look. "Don't jinx me, man! Don't say that."

"Fine," I said. "Whatever."

"Break a leg," Uncle said helpfully. "That's what you're supposed to say."

"Yo, thanks. Uncle gets it. He's dope. He's my number one fan."

I thought but did not add, "He's your only fan." Instead I curled up on the corner of the sofa with my paperback and bit my tongue.

On the third day, I was at work in the donut shop when the phone call came for Uncle. Anita answered the phone. "Why, no, sugar, he's not here right now, but this is La Petite Pâtisserie Khmère. Can I help you?"

I knew something was up immediately, because nobody called it that except Uncle. Nobody but Uncle and me in the letter to the reporter.

"Why, he should be in later this morning. He's usually back a little before noon."

I listened eagerly to Anita's end of the conversation, but it was mostly affirmations, "Mm-hmm," and "Yes, that's right," and then driving directions.

She turned to me. "Strangest thing. A reporter from the newspaper called. He wants to interview James."

"All right!" I slapped my hand against the countertop triumphantly. "I knew we could get them interested! I told the reporter we're having a Grand Opening. So if anyone asks, tell them that. For the New Year. For the training program. We can make up an excuse. When we started the Palace in Nebraska, Ma had a new Grand Opening every time she changed the menu or needed to get some new customers in." I took off my apron and hung it on a hook on the wall. "I better run over to Copy Circle and make some signs."

"Did you tell your Uncle?"

"No, it was going to be a surprise."

Anita nodded. For a second I worried that she might be upset, that she might not understand, but then she only winked at me good-naturedly. "Well, you're quite the businesswoman. You know, this might be just the thing James needs. I better call him and make sure he comes back here before the reporter arrives."

"Thanks, Anita!" I grabbed my jacket from the kitchen and ran out the back door. The sunlight seemed particularly bright. I'd never realized the sky was quite this blue, like a cerulean ocean, unbroken by any cloud. The pale gray pigeons pecking for garbage in the parking lot scattered as I ran past. They floated into the air like large, well-fed doves. It was a beautiful day. My scheme was working perfectly. This was going to be the best Christmas ever, I just knew it.

By the time the reporter arrived, we were ready. I'd put up a "Grand Opening" banner across the front window. I couldn't afford the all-weather version, so I'd had it printed on regular paper and hung it on the inside. Anita had called Sitan and managed to get him to mop the front room and clean all the windows. I wiped down all the counters and rearranged the pastry case for maximum appeal while Anita piled her hair up on her head in a massive bun with a pair of shellacked chopsticks sticking in the back and re-applied her makeup in the bathroom. When she re-emerged, she looked spectacular, like she must have in her knife-throwing days, like a real badass. She even convinced Uncle to go back to the apartment and put on a suit. When he returned, I was shocked at how well he'd cleaned up. He'd only worn a suit once before that I'd ever seen, when he was trying to convince some Chinese gangsters from Omaha to buy our restaurant, but he'd been nervous then, exhausted, and the suit had been too large. It hung on his frame, and he'd looked merely desperate, and the gangsters hadn't bought the restaurant in the end.

Then I remembered. Once upon a time I'd seen a black-and-white photograph of our family from before the war. I was just a toddler in it, dressed to match my mother, with a bow in my hair. The handsome father in the picture had been unrecognizable to me, nothing like the man I called Uncle, who looked old and tired and had missing teeth. I was used to seeing Uncle look haggard, in work clothes, dark circles under his eyes, smelling of restaurant oil and the prep station. But in the photograph, Uncle was wearing a Western suit that fit just right over his shoulders. His hair was thick and black and shiny with pomade. He had all his teeth and he'd looked as handsome as a movie star.

Now, as Anita adjusted Uncle's tie, I caught a glimpse of the man from the photograph. He looked prosperous and intellectual, like the man he'd once been before Pol Pot, like somebody who'd gone to university and hadn't expected to work with his hands over hot oil the rest of his life. And the thought came to me that it wasn't just because this suit fit better, but rather it was the way he looked at Anita as she brushed the lint off his shoulders. His face was relaxed, calm, pleased even. It occurred to me that Uncle might be in love with Anita and that she probably loved him, and that they hadn't wanted me to see this right off the bat. They felt the need to hide from me, as though I represented something uncomfortable for both of them, and that my showing up might have inconvenienced them or at least complicated their relationship in ways I couldn't quite understand.

It wasn't like I cared if Uncle remarried. It wasn't like I'd report back to Ma. And even if I did, did Uncle think she shouldn't know?

Before I could contemplate this new situation, the reporter showed up, and we all put on our happy smiling faces and there wasn't anything more for me to observe.

CHAPTER 9

The Good News

That Sunday the article about Uncle made the front page: "Khmer Rouge Survivor Revives Sweet Culture." It was a fluff piece, sentimental, and absolutely the kind of publicity I was hoping for. The article ran below the fold, which was a disappointment, but it was accompanied on the front page by a large photo of Uncle holding a tray of pastry, smiling and looking prosperous in his nice suit. There were a couple of smaller pictures on the jump page: the outside of the donut shop and a group shot of Uncle, Anita, Sitan, me, and three of the women who worked nights in Uncle's trainee program learning to make donuts and pastry. I was just a tiny dot in the background of the photo, but I folded the whole article up neatly and pressed it into my notebook.

Anita and Sitan were thrilled. Anita said she was going to buy a frame and put the article up on the wall of the donut shop, and Sitan circled his own face with a red pen and drew an arrow pointing to the Snugli hanging around his neck. He wrote his daughter's name in the margin.

"When you're famous, you'll have to come back and autograph this for us!" Anita said to him, and Sitan beamed.

Uncle, for his part, was silent. He kept the shop open only from eight to one on Sundays, for the before and after church business, but he stayed for the whole shift, chewing Nicorette and popping Sudafed tablets to stay awake. I'd been observing him for a nearly a week, and I'd figured out some of his tricks for keeping alert and working so much. I hoped the article made him proud, or at least pleased that his business was getting some recognition, but he didn't say anything. His old customers smiled at him and told him they'd seen him in the paper. Some said they didn't know he was a Khmer Rouge survivor, how it was terrible he'd lost his family. He thanked them, but I couldn't tell if he was happy or merely polite, or, worse, deep down a little anxious from the attention.

When it was time to close, Anita announced that they'd made double their usual take for a Sunday.

"Must be because of the article," I said, fishing for a compliment. "Good thing I wrote that reporter."

"He did a really good job," Sitan said. "Kept it real."

"Such a lovely photograph of James!" Anita nodded. "I don't know why the paper never thought to run an article before now."

"Yeah, they need to step up their reporting," Sitan said. "This community's got stories. You want to cry, I could tell you some stories. For real, man."

Then Uncle said that to celebrate he was going to take us all out to eat.

And, for the first time all morning, I relaxed a little bit, the tension in my neck and shoulders releasing just a tad. I hadn't realized how tightly I'd been holding myself, as though waiting to see how Uncle would react were a physical act, like carrying a heavy weight or lifting barbells above my head. Seeing that Uncle wanted to celebrate, I knew that he'd decided the article was a good thing; seeing Anita and Sitan happy had made him happy. Up until that moment, I wasn't sure how he felt, and perhaps he hadn't been sure either.

Uncle drove us to a small Mexican restaurant, El Patio, where the owner knew Uncle's name and greeted him with a smile and a clap on the back. "We haven't seen you in a while, James," the man said. "Then I see you in the paper today! Congratulations!"

"It's a lucky day," Uncle said, smiling.

The man led us to a big booth in the back underneath a wreath of chili peppers on the wall. Christmas carols played in Spanish over the sound system. The room smelled of smoke and chilies, cigarettes and salsa. It was bustling and friendly and the whole family seemed to be working there: from the bored teenage girl at the cash register to the boys carrying the trays and the little kid sitting on a stool spinning round and round at the counter. The place reminded me of the Palace, and I felt a twinge of homesickness.

At the Palace, the twins liked to plant themselves at the cash register up front so they could greet all the customers— said it gave them opportunities to practice their beauty queen smiles—but Sam had taken to working in the kitchen, refusing to come out. Ever since he'd given up wrestling, he'd become withdrawn, solitary, silent. He sat at the prep counter, television propped on a shelf with the volume blaring, as he watched the high school wrestling matches from out of state and all those ads for the army, promising a band of brothers. No wonder my lonely brother wanted to enlist.

While waiting for our food to arrive, Uncle and Anita shared a cigarette and Sitan told jokes about some of his club gigs—the rowdy crowds, the times he'd had to escape quickly, running through the parking lot because he thought he'd be robbed. He spoke as though these tough times were long behind him, as though he were already a star reminiscing about the hard early days, able to laugh now because those days were distant and over.

I wondered—if Sam ever met Sitan, could they become friends? Was this the kind of buddy he needed? Maybe he wouldn't have to leave us and become a soldier, moving to a base overseas, if he only had a friend here he could confide in.

It was funny how a little bit of good luck, a little bit of good news, could make everybody feel fortunate and optimistic. Even me. Sitting in the red vinyl booth next to Anita and Sitan, watching Uncle smile as he drew on one of Anita's cigarettes and then released the smoke in a long, languid cloud, I could believe that we'd turned a bend in our bad luck, in our difficult times, and that from now on things would only get better and better.

On Monday morning business was booming at the donut shop. Because of the article, we were a curiosity, something to be experienced and discussed. We were hot.

We sold out of everything by the time the noon lunch crowd rolled in. Some of the regulars were disappointed that they couldn't get their usual donuts. Anita whistled. "The after-work crowd is not going to like this."

I had no sympathy. "Tell them to come in the morning next time, before they go to work," I said. "We can sell out even faster that way. Maybe we can start taking advance orders."

Sitan brought out a bag of donut holes that he'd put aside. "It's been so busy, I didn't have time to eat breakfast," he said. "But I saved us some."

Anita popped one in her mouth. "My hero!"

Out of politeness, I took a small bite, but to my surprise the dough tasted sweet instead of dusty this time, like a fresh lychee—light and tasty and exactly what I'd craved.

I brought out my notebook while they snacked.

"If business keeps up, we'll have to expand production. Maybe some of the bakers could come in and start another batch of donuts before the after-school and after-work crowds. Also, we could jazz up the menu and start passing out samples while we're still attracting all the curiosity seekers. Maybe offer picnic lunches to go. What do you think?"

Sitan grew excited. "I had these ideas. You know, kinda make a special flavor of the month? Like Super Fly Chocolate Love and D.J. Fresh Flava Spice. You know, something I can relate to."

"That's great," I said, scribbling his suggestions down. I wasn't about to quash his enthusiasm. He could work out the details, like the actual flavors, later. "I'm putting you down for coming up with new names."

Anita traced the outline of her tattoo on her arm. "I've always wanted to explore the tastes of Cambodia. Maybe do a savory donut. Like cardamom. Or tarragon. Maybe a hot pepper donut." Anita licked the sugar off her fingers one by one.

"Fantastic!" I said. "Maybe you and Sitan could collaborate?"

Anita took the pencil off her ear and started writing on a paper napkin. "We could do just a small batch to begin. Maybe I'll start small at home so I don't ruin anything."

"I bet anything you come up with the bakers could design a special icing for. Or a special shape."

Anita nodded, enthused. "They're real artists. James found two women, the Kasim sisters, who were trained by French pastry chefs before Pol Pot. I bet they could create something unique."

"Great! I'll let you explain to Uncle what you want to do. In the meantime, I'll design a flyer with some coupons for today. When the after-school crowd comes, even if we don't have enough donuts to sell them, we don't want to turn anyone away empty-handed. I'll give them a flyer so they'll want to come back tomorrow."

"You a business major, college girl?" Sitan asked. "They teach you all this stuff?"

"No, I have *real* experience. My mother tried everything with our restaurant in Nebraska. I learned from her."

Then, high from our sugar break, we all set to work. Sitan cleaned up, Anita got a hold of the Kasim sisters, who agreed to come in to work on another batch, and I went over to the Copy Circle and started designing a flyer. All-New Flavor of the Month. Super Fly Flavor of the Week. Secret Flavor Preview! Delicioso Donut of the Day. Mekong Melt in Your Mouth. Naga Magic Eclair. Apsaras Heavenly Cream. I kept trying different combinations of words, wondering if I could find the perfect one that would entice customers. That would make the business a success. That would make Uncle proud of me. The way my plans were working out, I could almost imagine calling the reporter next week with the big reveal: the return of the lost daughter, the family reunion that should land us a story above the fold.

By the time I came back to the shop with a test batch of flyers, two of the bakers had arrived. Anita introduced me to the Kasim sisters. They were Cham Muslims who'd survived the Khmer Rouge, she said, even though most of their family had not. They'd been sponsored by a Catholic church in Fresno, but moved down here after discovering a cousin working in the Inland Empire. They were putting their aprons over their clothes, but still wore colorful checked *krama* scarves draped over their hair. They smiled at me as I greeted them in the kitchen.

I pulled on a white apron. "I'll help. Just let me know what you need me to do."

They tittered behind their hands. "Mademoiselle, you can watch and stay out of our way."

They floured the counter and set to work, bringing the bowls of butter out of the refrigerator, and I realized they were going to make another batch of pastry, not donuts, which excited me. I'd wanted to raise the prices on the pastry, and now, with everything else sold out, this would be the perfect opportunity.

Even as the heat rose in the kitchen—despite the three fans blowing full-force and the back door open with another fan wedged in the jamb to suck out more of the hot air—the sisters did not seem to break a sweat. They conferred with each other, speaking in low voices, their black eyes fixed on the pastry dough that they rolled and shaped on the wooden cutting boards.

I helped Sitan wash the mixing bowls, the blades, the spoons, the icing bags and tips, and the chopping boards while Anita waited out front, serving coffee to all the new people who happened by, drawn by the newspaper article. She remembered to pass out my flyers urging customers to come back again to try our special flavors—changed daily! I'd written, figuring I was only exaggerating a little—while promising that a new batch of pastry would be ready by five.

I could just imagine Uncle's face when he came in after his trip to the hospital, where he was still acting as a translator for a sick family. How excited he'd be to see the donut shop actually crowded with paying customers, people who appreciated his pastries, the throngs at the counter, the line out the door. How happy and surprised he'd be. I'd try to act modest, to defer all the compliments, to remember to share the praise with Sitan and Anita and the Kasim sisters. I'd tell him about phase two of the plan, how we'd use this week or two of special attention to plant the seeds for long-term customers. We'd keep building on the momentum, week after week, until we were the best donut shop in the city. I could get restaurant critics from bigger papers to come by. I'd issue invitations, we could sponsor events, maybe host late-nights when we stayed open just to launch a new flavor. We'd create a brand name. Uncle could afford to open a second location, and we could renovate the shop—spruce up the front so it didn't have to look old and sad. We could make it look like Phnom Penh as Anita remembered it, before the war. We could add a pretty sign. Sitan would have his own franchise and maybe his girlfriend would come back and marry him. I could work here full time; I could move to California, establish residency; maybe I could get my sisters to go here for college, too. Even Sam might decide not to enlist straight out of high school, and instead move out to work here and find a friend.

But I was getting ahead of myself, drunk on dreams of happiness. That was dangerous, I knew.

I focused on washing the mixing bowl in my hands, letting the hot water slosh over the stiff dough, the soapsuds breaking down the flour and butter, and rubbing the sides with the scrubber until the metal gleamed. Still, I couldn't help but feel I was rubbing a magic lamp, the kind with a cartoon genie that popped out to grant me wishes. My heart felt that light and free.

Business was booming the whole week after the newspaper article ran. Uncle was ecstatic, but not quite in the way I'd expected. "Everyone has read the article. Everyone. And everyone shared with me their own stories."

"Father Juan showed it around the homeless shelter?" Anita smiled.

"And at the hospital the nurses and the doctors saw it. At the youth center, the battered women's center, the free clinic, everyone read it. Everywhere I go, everyone wants to tell me what happened to them, too." Uncle shook his head as though he couldn't believe his good fortune.

He told us that from the hospice rounds to the food bank to the daycare center, all the other refugees wanted to tell him what had happened to their own families under the Khmer Rouge, how their children had died, or their parents, or their families. How they heard the dead crying in their dreams, weeping on the wind, wailing in the dead of night.

How horrible, I thought.

But Uncle was overjoyed. Everyone was talking to him, telling him their troubles, sharing what they hadn't wanted to say before, when he'd seemed like a lucky man who'd escaped before the Khmer Rouge took over, like a man who wasn't like them, a man who couldn't possibly understand.

I'd wanted Uncle to see the donut shop as a success. I'd wanted him to see what a good businesswoman I was and be impressed and proud. Not this.

"There is so much suffering in the world," Uncle said. "There is so much suffering among my people. But today I know I was spared for a reason. I will devote myself to helping them all."

I hadn't imagined Uncle's survivor's guilt could get any worse. I was wrong.

I was mopping up the sticky floor, sloshing suds of Pine-Sol across the tile. Hearing Uncle talk, I wondered if he even remembered that I was the one who'd written the press release, called the newspaper, found the reporter who'd written the story in the first place.

Was I somehow the one thing about the past that should remain forgotten?

Nursing my sense of martyrdom like a scab I couldn't stop picking, I mopped furiously, attacking the grime that I had once mistaken for an actual pattern on the tile. Gradually the floor lightened by three shades, from a deep dusty dirt color to a pale vanilla.

Sitan emerged from the back, where he'd been washing the last of the trays. "I'm gonna head out. Congratulations, Uncle," he said. "This has been the best week ever."

"Funny how a little PR works magic," I said bitterly.

"We should buy a tree," Uncle said. "It's almost Christmas. We should celebrate."

I looked around the front room, thinking about the needles that would fall all over the floor. "No space."

"Oh, a tree! A live tree! Wouldn't that be lovely?" Anita beamed. "We should put it in that corner. Right under the 'Open' sign."

"Yeah! We could get some lights, really fix it up. It's Lillian's first Christmas. She'd like that."

I sighed but didn't argue. Thinking about a tree made me feel sour inside. Another reminder that I'd chosen to spend my Christmas away from my family. The rituals didn't feel the same away from them. The twins always competed to see who could create the more lavish tree decorations, dividing the tree in half and draping shiny garlands and strings of popcorn, metallic balls and silvery icicles and clothespin angels through the thick green boughs. In Texas, Ma hadn't celebrated Christmas when I was little, but as the twins entered junior high, they only remembered life in America. They couldn't imagine celebrating without a tree, the same way they couldn't imagine answering to anything but their American names—Jennifer and Marie instead of Navy and Maly—and Ma couldn't deny them. One year they'd glued Chinese crispy noodles spray-painted gold onto construction-paper rings and enveloped the tree as though it were one of the "Chinese salads" they'd concocted to compete with the McDonald's that had opened in the next town over. Sam was a good big brother to them, humoring their little-girl whims. He set up the ladder and held it tight as they put up the various angels at the very top—blonde angels with gossamer rings, pink-haired fairies, a red-headed mermaid, and one year a Cambodian *devata*, complete with gold tiara. Now my little sisters were teenagers, fifteen, and Sam would turn eighteen soon, old enough to enlist. Yet here I was in California. When would we celebrate Christmas together again as a family? I wondered if I'd been foolish to come here.

As it was so late in the season, just eight days before Christmas, we soon discovered that most of the tree lots had sold out long ago. Uncle drove us by all the grocery stores—Lucky's and A&P and Kroger's—but there were only a few spindly wreaths left, some shedding poinsettias, and no live trees, although the big Chinese grocery Lion's had a few artificial trees, including a small counter model spray-painted pink. But Uncle insisted now that we should have a real tree.

One of the clerks at Lion's took pity on us and said he thought some people were selling trees from their lawn in town. It was one of the small houses with lots of lights. That sounded like any house to me, but Uncle thanked him, and the four of us piled back into Uncle's Toyota and took off through the back streets, following an array of Christmas decorations so bright that it seemed as though some people were personally trying to guide a jumbo jet into a safe landing in their driveway. I saw houses coated in fake snow and electric icicles and guarded by lit-from-within giant plastic snowmen. One intrepid family had sprayed their entire green lawn with what looked like shaving cream and spider webs, trying to mimic snow. Another had managed to string lights in the palm tree on their lawn. They'd also constructed a manger strung with blinking lights and accompanied by animated wise men who waved beside a pair each of donkeys, camels, zebras, and elephants. Their Bible references were decidedly mixed, combining the Nativity with Noah's Ark, but Sitan was thrilled. He held Lillian up from her baby seat. "Look, Lillian, look! See all the animals!"

Finally we came upon a small house set far from the street, at the end of a cul-de-sac where the houses grew more sparse and the orange groves lined both sides of the street. Two spotlights shone upon a motley collection of pine trees tied to stakes on the crabgrass lawn. A dog barked furiously from inside the house. A hand-painted sign hung on the garage door: "Trees 4 Sale."

"Looks like they just went up to Big Bear Mountain and chopped them down themselves," Anita said.

"Is that legal?" I asked, but nobody cared.

We pulled into the driveway and got out to inspect the trees. There was one pine that wasn't quite as spare and straggly-looking as the others. We pulled on the needles and they didn't all fall off in our hands. A woman in a bathrobe emerged from the squat house and we asked, How much for the tree? She said forty, and I said twenty, and then she sold it to us for thirty. Sitan strapped it on the roof with bungee cords from the trunk, and we drove back to the donut shop with our Christmas tree.

That night we stayed up late decorating the tree with ornaments that we got from the Asian grocery, thirty percent off since they knew us. The bakers came in, and the Kasim sisters smiled to see our sturdy pine before the front window. They said they'd bake us an angel out of sugar-cookie dough, something special, and they hummed carols as they worked. After they finished their first batch, they came out from the kitchen and sang a song together in French while the cookies baked. I didn't know the words, but the tune was nice, better than Rudolph or Frosty or all the other kids' songs I was used to hearing blare from the loudspeakers at the strip mall.

Soon the donut shop filled with the scent of baking dough and sugar and pine tree. While the tree hadn't seemed like much propped up on that woman's lawn, it revived once we set it up and put a pan of water under the trunk.

"Those mountain pines are the best," Anita said. "Just breathe in! Smells better than those sickly trees sitting out in those lots all month!"

Indeed, our possibly poached tree did smell wonderful, like mountain air and sunshine and a Southern California winter. Sitan held Lillian in his arms and helped her hang tinsel on the branches, then pulled the tinsel out of her mouth as she tried to eat it. Anita gave her some clothespin reindeer to hang instead.

Finally Uncle came out, handprints in flour on the knees of his khakis. He looked at the tree, he looked at Anita smiling and Sitan playing with Lillian, and he held up a sugar cookie. "Look what the Kasim sisters made for the tree!"

It was an Apsaras, a dancing girl with curvy hips and full breasts and gracefully extended arms. It was the sexiest-looking Christmas ornament ever.

"Those are awesome!" Sitan exclaimed. "I wanna eat one!"

"We can poke a hole in the tiara and hang this right here." Anita pulled at a bare branch. "If they make a batch, we can cover the tree."

"If they make a batch, we can sell these for five bucks a piece!" I said. "We can launch a whole new line of products. These are the homage to Cambodian culture we've been looking for. Get some icing, draw on a face, these would really sell."

They looked at me as though I'd started barking like a dog.

"Yes, I mean, they're beautiful for the tree. Sure," I said. "But we shouldn't waste them on the tree. We should sell these!"

Uncle looked a little startled. "It's Christmas. This is supposed to be a religious holiday. Everything shouldn't be about money."

I wondered how on earth he could have lived in America all these years and still think that way. I opened my mouth, but before I could say anything, Anita put a hand on my arm.

"I know exactly what James is saying." Anita took the cookie and held it to a branch. "This is a gift for the tree from the Kasim sisters. And we can hang it right here." She smiled at Uncle gently, and he nodded. Then she turned to me. "And if they want to make any more, we can follow Nea's idea. Later."

I didn't say anything more. There didn't seem to be any point, since I clearly didn't understand at all.

PART FOUR

If you see a tiger sleeping, don't assume it's dead.

—traditional Cambodian proverb

CHAPTER 10

The Gangster

Our Christmas tree with the sexy ornaments was a big hit. I was a little worried the next morning when a couple of cops came in for a coffee break—I was afraid they'd be able to tell we had a poached tree—but once they took a look at the Apsaras cookies, they didn't even notice the pine tree underneath.

"You gonna sell these kind of cookies?" one asked.

"We might. Come back next week and find out," I said.

Since Uncle had worked through the night supervising the bakers, he slept through the morning rush, when all three of us were waiting on customers, Anita barely able to ring up each sale fast enough before another customer pushed to the front of the line clutching a pink box full of pastry. Then he didn't come in for the noon rush either.

All week, we'd had great crowds, but Uncle never saw any of them. I wondered if this were part of his penance or if he were trying to avoid me, or if, perhaps, he really enjoyed his rounds more than standing behind the counter ringing up sales. I was pleased with the success, but I was already growing a little restless. The donut shop wasn't as interesting as running our restaurant at home. I was more of a cashier than anything else here.

Still, every time I heard the bells on the door ring, I glanced up and peered over the crowd at the counter, hoping I'd spot Uncle coming in, but it was never him.

As our trays were depleted and we had to turn some customers away, I called out, "Come back tomorrow bright and early! We'll have plenty more!"

Sitan laughed at me, but I said, "Hey, don't let a potential customer get away. We need as many people as we can get."

"Aye, aye, Captain." He saluted me with a wink.

Then the bells rang again, and I looked up eagerly. This time it was a surly-looking Asian man in his early twenties, his hair shaved close on the sides, the top spiked high. He wore a white short-sleeved T-shirt and had dense tats on both arms. My first thought was, Gangster. He's casing the place. I gave him a hard look, the kind that said, I remember what you look like, and he looked away, rubbing his arms as though he thought he could hide the tigers and snakes and dragons emblazoned there.

I tried to nudge Sitan, I wanted him to see, too, just in case, but Sitan was busy flirting with a nurse in scrubs as he rang up her bag of donut holes. Anita had disappeared, maybe she'd slipped into the back to take a bathroom break, maybe she was getting something from the kitchen. I hoped the gangbanger had seen her when he'd come in so that he knew we had a white person working in here, someone the cops would care about if he tried to rob us. I knew I shouldn't think this way—the counselor I went to see in college would have labeled this a low self-esteem issue—but I thought it all the same. This is what I would call my survival instinct.

I made a mental note to myself to send a flyer to the police station. If any more cops should come by, we should offer them free coffee with a donut purchase. We should print up a coupon for them, something their families could bring in later. I'd have to train everyone to smile and say, "Thank you for stopping by, officers." I needed to re-think my issues with authority figures.

A steady stream of cops coming in for a sugar and caffeine fix would be better than hiring a private security guard.

As we were close to closing, our customers had thinned until there were just some teenagers checking each other out while pretending to look at the drinks in the cooler. Sitan was ringing up a woman and her daughter coming back from soccer practice.

The mother laughed with her daughter, and they waved their good-byes.

"Keep checking back!" I called. "We're changing our menu all the time!"

Anita emerged from the kitchen and pinched me on the arm. "You little capitalist. Can't stop the sales pitch, can you?"

I shook my head. Now that Anita was back, I was hoping the gangbanger would take notice and leave. But he was hanging back by the booth, waiting for the teenagers to finish paying for their drinks.

Anita came up behind me and leaned her chin into my shoulder. "Are you thinking what I'm thinking?" she whispered into my ear. "That guy's been staring at you for about fifteen minutes."

"Don't say anything." I kept my face neutral. "He won't try anything so long as you're here. At least, I don't think he would."

"Don't worry, sweetie. I won't embarrass you." She winked at me. "I think he's cute, too."

I stared at Anita in amazement. With a nod, she licked her finger and touched my thigh, then pulled back as though she'd burned herself.

She's going to be no help at all, I thought.

Then the teenagers left and the gangbanger made his move. He stepped forward toward the cash register, without even bothering to pretend to want to buy anything.

"Excuse me," the gangbanger said softly. He reached under his shirt into the back pocket of his baggy jeans and I thought, This is it, he's got a gun, he's going to hold us up, and dammit, on the very first week we start making real money. I tried to think of something I could do, like pretend to get him a donut and pull out a tray and hit him with it instead, but then he pulled out a newspaper clipping. He unfolded it, smoothed it on the counter, and I saw it was the story about Uncle. The gangbanger pointed to Uncle's smiling face in the picture. "This man, the owner, I'd like to see him."

I bet you would, I thought. "Why?" I demanded.

"He sure is the owner, sugar," Anita said. "But he's not in right now."

The gangbanger looked disappointed. His shoulders slumped, and I wondered why he would need to rob the owner in particular. "I came all the way from L.A."

"L.A.! My goodness, that's a drive! Well, don't feel bad, sug'. He should be here any minute. He usually stops in to help close up. Why don't you have a seat and wait?" She pointed to the booth, and the gangbanger nodded and went to take his seat.

I couldn't believe how dense Anita was. She offered the wannabe thief some coffee, then tea. We only had a few jellyrolls left that Sitan had dropped on the kitchen floor. They'd exploded, breaking open so the jelly squirted out, but Sitan had picked them up quickly and set them aside so we could eat them ourselves later. Now I heard Anita calling them "a kitchen accident" as she offered one to the gangbanger. "They're still delicious," she said.

"Anita," I grabbed the cuff of her blouse. "You don't know what you're doing."

"Oh, yes I do," she said. "He's just shy. Look how he's looking at you, girl! He's just working up his nerve to make his move."

"That's what I'm afraid of," I said, but Anita wouldn't listen. She picked up the broom and made as though to leave us alone while she went to sweep up the paper and soda cans and cigarette butts and other crap that people left littered in front of the shop.

Then Sitan popped out of the kitchen, carrying his duffel bag. "Is it okay if I take off? I should pick up my girl from the sitter."

"Wait, Uncle's not here yet!" I said.

"Go ahead, Sitan. You've worked more than a full day, sweetheart."

"But I need you to help me clean up!" I cried out. I could not believe that Anita was going to leave us alone and vulnerable. I didn't know how to explain it, but I could sense there was something odd about this gang guy. My arms were covered with goosepimples, as though a cold wind were suddenly blowing through the shop. "Can't you stay, Sitan?"

"Okay, sure, Nea." Sitan put down his duffel, but Anita picked it up and put it in his hand. "I'll help tonight. Go ahead and go. Scoot now!"

Sitan smiled, waved, and headed out the door.

Then Anita disappeared into the kitchen.

At this point, alone with the gangbanger, I wondered if it wasn't fated that I should die ironically in a meaningless robbery in my own father's donut shop in a failed and pathetic attempt to get him to acknowledge me.

Yet the gangster made no moves. He continued to sit in the booth, sipping his coffee and eating the remains of the jellyroll. He had surprisingly good table manners and didn't leave crumbs all over the Formica like other customers, but brushed them up with a napkin.

I decided there was no point in my being a martyr, so I bundled up the trash and left the gangster alone in the shop.

If he wanted to rob us, let him. I carried the Hefty bag to the dumpster on the far edge of the parking lot. It was completely dark now, the night air cold. It wasn't Nebraska cold—I certainly would have considered it a heat wave if it were in the forties in December back home—but I'd grown used to the thick sunshine of Santa Bonita during the day. Now that the sun had set, there were only the pale yellow puddles from the lights in the parking lot and the cacophony of blinking Christmas lights along the strip mall. I shivered as my breath pooled before my head like an empty thought bubble.

A stream of cars pulled into the lot. The lights flashed against the dumpster, the cars turned round the bend, and I thought, This is it, the gangbanger's accomplices, but then some of the cars pulled up to the grocery, and others rattled over the speed bumps and headed out the back exit to the alley, trying to avoid the traffic on the main street. The hair stood up on my arms, and I realized I was chilled and foolish to be standing outside waiting for disaster. I tossed the Hefty bag and ran back to the donut shop.

The gangster was still seated in the booth. He held his head in his hands, his eyes closed, his lips moving as though he were rehearsing something, and I wondered if he was practicing his line that this was a holdup.

Then, as though he could read my thoughts, he opened his eyes and stared directly at me.

It was creepy, the way he looked at me. Startled and intense at the same time. As though I frightened him for some reason. Maybe he could tell I had him figured out, I thought.

Anita offered him some more coffee.

I shook my head and went about wiping down the counters.

After another half hour, the gangster got tired of waiting. He nodded at Anita and thanked her for the coffee and the exploded jellyroll, then left a dollar tip on the tabletop when she said the coffee was on the house. He folded the clipping back into his pocket and walked back into the dark parking lot.

"You think he's coming back?" Anita peered through the window into the dark. "Poor fellow. Drove all that way."

"That's weird, Anita. It's not a good sign." I locked the door and flipped the sign on the window to "Closed."

Finally, after another fifteen minutes, which felt like thirty, Uncle returned. I watched his headlights flash against the front door as he parked. He bounded in the front door.

"I had the best day," he beamed. He told Anita eagerly about a family he'd helped. The grandfather had complained of chest pain, but the doctors couldn't find anything wrong with his heart. The man kept telling his family that a ghost was sitting on his chest, and Uncle had recognized this as a sign of PTSD and had been able to translate for the man so that he was able to see a specialist to help with his anxiety. In the meantime, the family was going to contact a monk and see if a ceremony could be performed for the man's wife, who had died under Pol Pot. "The man felt so guilty, he was certain his wife's ghost was visiting him at night, sitting on his chest." After Uncle spoke to him, the man admitted that he was afraid his wife was lost in the netherworld, unable to find her way to Hell, where she'd be able to be judged and re-enter the cycle of samsara. "I told him the monks would be able to chant her soul back to sleep. He shouldn't worry anymore. We will help him."

After he told all this to Anita, it felt trivial to brag to him about our great sales. Or to berate him for coming back so late. Or to mention the gangster who'd driven from L.A. Although he'd spooked me, now that I'd had time to think about it, I realized the man was probably just looking for a job.

"I feel I am finally able to help people," Uncle said, his face slightly sweaty, his eyes aglow from a light burning inside him.

"Did you remember to eat?" Anita asked. "I've told you, you can't just live on my Nicorette and black coffee all day long."

Uncle nodded, blinking as though he were waking from a long and beautiful dream. "We should eat. Yes," he said. "Are you hungry? It's dark." He looked out the windows as though noticing for the first time that the whole day had passed. Then he announced that he'd take us to Denny's. He went to use the bathroom while we waited.

I pulled the plug on the Christmas lights. I didn't want the whole tree to go up in flames while we were out. I traced one of the Apsaras cookies. I wished I could send some home to the twins. My sisters would like these ornaments, I knew, although Ma might find them too racy. Thinking about my family, I felt a little lonely again.

"Cheer up, honey. I bet he'll be back tomorrow," Anita said, startling me. She'd come up behind me and I hadn't noticed.

"I'm not interested in that gang guy," I said.

Anita raised an eyebrow, but didn't push the issue. "You know, James is very happy to have you here."

"No, he's not!" The anger I felt surprised me.

"Honey, he's not very good at talking about his feelings. He's doing his best."

"Yes," I said, wishing she'd stop making excuses for him.

"You've worked so hard since you got here. You've really turned business around. This is the happiest I've ever seen James. This is the first year since his wife died that he's had a tree or put up any decorations. I think he was punishing himself. He blamed himself for her death, you know."

"Wait, you knew Auntie?"

"I met them when they first opened. I needed a job and they hired me."

I hadn't realized Anita had known my birth mother. I felt suddenly more exposed. She knew things about Auntie that I didn't. Maybe she knew things about me, too. But then I shook my head. I didn't think Auntie would confide in a stranger. She was too damaged, too embittered. Maybe if she'd had someone she could confide in, she wouldn't have overdosed.

"Your uncle used to work in the donut shop around the clock," Anita continued. "It was a different place in those days. He made the donuts himself. He cleaned the place night and day, he kept it spic and span, but it wasn't like now. I don't mean to criticize, don't get me wrong, but it wasn't exactly a happy place. Then when his wife passed away, James blamed himself. He was at work when it happened. He didn't find her until too late."

"There was nothing he could have done. She'd tried to kill herself before."

"But he did blame himself. After that, it was like he hated himself for being alive. He won't say it, but he's been suffering ever since. If God wouldn't punish him, he'd punish himself. But now he's changing. He's got a purpose. He's happier. You've made him feel this way."

I sighed. Anita didn't know the half of it. For all I could tell, Uncle was manically spending his time with other people to avoid me. But I didn't know how to tell her this. I didn't know how to explain all that had passed in our family, all the complications. And I didn't want to betray my own quixotic dreams, didn't want to be disappointed or exposed or both. Somehow, voicing my desire for acceptance made me feel naive and stupid, like someone who could be lied to, someone who could be hurt, again and again and again. I didn't know how to explain that I wanted to wait for the right moment, a safe moment, when I knew that Uncle was truly proud of me, and that I was truly worthy of love. Only then would I tell him that I knew his secret, my secret. Our secret. If I chose the wrong moment, I was sure I'd ruin everything.

"Ready to go?" Uncle asked behind us, emerging from the kitchen doors.

Anita put a too-bright smile on her face. "You bet, sugar! We were just saying how hungry we were."

I thought, What a rotten actress Anita is, but I was genuinely impressed at how quickly she tried to mask her own feelings and put Uncle at ease. For his part, Uncle pretended to believe her.

I wished I had their energy for cheerful dissembling, but I didn't.

CHAPTER 11

The Homecoming

On Sunday morning, Uncle made breakfast for me, still buoyed by his happy feelings from the night before. He made French omelettes with toast and very thick black coffee, but I noticed he didn't eat. He pushed his eggs around his plate, took a handful of Sudafed with his black coffee, stuck more Nicorette in his pocket, and returned to work. Anita and Sitan had the day off, so it was just him and me, but he didn't speak much to me. Instead he chatted with the customers, thanked them for coming, nodded when they told him stories about their own hard lives. Now that everyone knew the story of his suffering in the paper, people wanted to share, as though he were suddenly an expert in misery. They told him about failed marriages, broken homes, family fights, lost jobs, lost fortunes, lost dreams. He smiled and nodded, as though to say, I know exactly what you mean.

I looked around for the gangster, but he didn't come, and I felt relieved.

The next day, there was a large crowd for the 8:00 a.m. shift, even bigger than the previous week. Sitan greeted me with a smile, waving from behind the counter as he rung up another customer. I had quickly dropped off my backpack in the kitchen, tied on an apron, and come out front, when I realized he was wearing his Snugli with his daughter in it. She burbled happily, blowing spit bubbles over her fist, which was wedged in her mouth.

That was probably a violation of some health code, I thought. I instinctively scanned the crowd, looking for disgruntled snitch faces, but everyone seemed focused on the pastry cases.

I was feeling grumpy and tired. I hadn't slept well. A week and a half on the sofa was taking its toll. I tried to muster a smile as I took my place behind the counter next to Sitan, who slapped me on the back enthusiastically. "Another boffo day!" he said. "Everybody wants their Cambo-Donuts!"

His daughter took her hand out of her mouth and crowed triumphantly, then socked me with a fist of saliva.

"Another great day," I agreed, stifling a yawn.

Then we turned back to the hungry crowd.

I was mentally on autopilot till noon, when, along with another wave of customers, Anita came in to take over for Sitan.

That was when I noticed that the gangbanger had returned. He was dressed the exact same as before, white T, baggy jeans, shades. He waited in the back of the crowd, watching, as he let everyone else step in front of him and order their pastry. I thought we should call the cops right now, even if it turned out to be a false alarm. I'd give them a dozen donuts to make up for it.

But before I could tell Anita my plan, the gangbanger took his spot at the counter and introduced himself.

"Hello," he said formally, "my name is Chhouen Ponleu. I go by Paul here. Is the owner in?" He pulled the clipping about Uncle from his back pocket and smoothed it against the counter top.

"No, he's not in." I kept my voice level and calm.

Anita, sensing I was nervous, stepped up beside me. "But you're right, that is James in the photograph. He usually comes in later in the day. Maybe we can help you?"

The gangster nodded. "James." He said the name softly, as though he were testing it out, like a gumdrop on his tongue, or a sourball, something he wasn't sure would taste good. "I need to see James. Can you tell him I am here?"

"You'll have to come back later. How about you leave your name and number, and when James comes back, he can give you a call."

The gangster's eyes watered, and he licked his lips. "I've come very far to see him."

"You looking for a job?" Anita's voice softened. She was too kindhearted. I was afraid she'd hire this guy on the spot, no questions asked. Then what would happen after we were robbed? Although even I had to admit, this gang guy was a little slow-moving if he intended to hold us up. He had the advantage, after all. The crowd was gone for the moment. He should've pulled his weapon by now. I wondered if might be on drugs, something that slowed him down and made him nervous. He was sweating, and he looked scared. I supposed that fear could precede violence, but his manner threw me. There were the tough-guy tats, but then the soft voice, the polite demeanor.

"Have you tried at the Church of Everlasting Sorrow? He's usually helping out in the soup kitchen in the afternoons. You can talk to the father and see when he expects James." Anita was writing down Father Juan's number on the back of a cash register receipt.

"Why do you want to see James?" I asked bluntly.

"He is my father," the gangster said.

"What?" I blinked.

He tried to say something fast in Khmer, but my Khmer was a child's language, and his was eloquent, sophisticated. I hadn't heard someone talk like this to me since I had to wait on Auntie. I didn't want to be confused. "You have to use English for Anita," I said, my heart beating too fast.

The young man nodded and stepped back, holding his hands at his side, as though he were a schoolboy called upon to recite a lesson. "I am Chhouen Ponleu. I am the owner's son from Cambodia. He is my father. I saw the picture in the paper. I almost couldn't believe my eyes. But I read the article over and over and I'm sure. It's him. His Khmer name is Chhouen Suoheng. He was married to my mother, Chhang Sopheam, in Phnom Penh in 1962. They had five children. I am the oldest son. When I was ten years old, the Khmer Rouge sent me away from my mother to another work camp. In the article in the newspaper it says I disappeared. But I am here now." He spoke without pausing for breath, as though he'd rehearsed his speech many times, the words like the dots and dashes of a special kind of Morse code.

Anita let out a loud squeal. "Oh, my god! My god!" She ran around the counter and hugged the young man. He seemed startled, blinking, as though he were trying to wake from a deep sleep and was not yet certain if he were still in a dream. "I must call your father right away! Oh, this is such a beautiful thing!" She hugged him tightly and started to cry. "He's been looking for you. He's been looking for you for years!"

"He looked for me?" The young man blinked.

"Oh, he sure did. I'm going to call him. Right now!" Anita reached over the counter and pulled the phone to her. She dialed quickly, then held the receiver tight as it rang at the other end. "Oh, Mrs. Garcia, is James there? . . . Not yet? You must tell him to come right back to the pâtisserie. Something important's come up. A miracle! . . . A young man is here to see him. Please tell him to come right away when you see him." She hung up. Then she squinted at the speed dial and tried another number.

I leaned against the back cabinet, the coffee pots percolating behind me and throwing heat against my skin, as Anita called all the possible places she thought Uncle might be. She left messages for him all across town.

I felt faint, neither happy nor sad, just shocked. I stared at this stranger in front of me, this young man staring shyly at the counter top. But maybe he wasn't shy, I thought. Maybe he's hiding his eyes. Maybe he was lying. But then I felt guilty. Why did I need to be cynical? Why couldn't I be happy? I'd come all this way to see Uncle again, to get to know my real father, to ask him to accept me as his daughter again, to find my family, and here was this young man claiming to be the older brother I thought had probably died under Pol Pot. I should have been overjoyed. In a movie, I would have cried and laughed at the same time. The actress who played me would have jumped up and down and thrown herself into her long-lost brother's arms. He would have spun her around and around, as they laughed with all their teeth showing. But I was shivering despite the heat from the coffee pots, both regular and decaf, hissing behind me.

I didn't remember him at all. Not one thing.

He must have been in the family picture. Auntie showed it to me exactly once, just before she and Uncle moved away from Nebraska to California. It was a beautiful photograph, like something out of a fairy tale, certainly not like anything I associated with my own life. The people in it were elegantly dressed, calm, perfect. I told Auntie she was beautiful, her skin silky-smooth, pale, her face round as the full moon, her black hair bobbed and permed in soft waves that framed her face. I'd barely glanced at the children. I'd been too startled to see my aunt looking whole and glamorous, nothing like the woman I knew, whose face was scarred, her soul dark.

This was before Sourdi told me that this woman was my birth mother.

In the picture, there had been a baby in a bassinet, two boys dressed in expensive clothes, and a girl with a bow in her hair. The eldest boy wore a Western-style suit—a jacket, a tie, a button-up shirt. I didn't remember his face. I hadn't looked carefully.

I'd been impressed by the fancy studio, the overstuffed divan upon which Auntie lounged, the beribboned bassinet to her right. It must have been taken shortly after my youngest brother was born. Uncle was wearing a suit that matched the eldest boy's.

This was all I remembered of the family that once was mine.

Should I quiz this man now? Should I say, Do you remember getting your photograph taken? What did you wear? Where did you stand? Whose hand did you hold? A trick question to trip him up.

The anger welling up inside my chest surprised me. I clenched my fists so tightly that my nails left dents in my palms and my fingers ached. I clenched my jaw, too, and my teeth hurt.

I felt as though I'd been thrown and had struck a wall, hard.

The young man watched eagerly as Anita talked on the phone, trying to track down Uncle. His face now unguarded, was eager, hopeful.

I wanted to hurt him then. I wanted to hit him for standing there and openly showing the hope for reunion that I'd been hiding deep inside my heart and never dared to reveal.

Here he'd come, and now I was nothing.

He was the lost son. I was the abandoned daughter.

Suddenly, I bent over double, my stomach seizing up. I crouched, then had to sit on the floor, my back against the cabinet, its knobs poking the sweaty flesh of my back. I felt hot and cold simultaneously. I couldn't support the weight of my head. I had to lie on the cool floor. I noticed the spots I'd missed with the mop, the dark collection of dirt and dust bunnies and bits of paper and chewed gum and crumbs and a bus ticket stuck together under the counter, where the mop couldn't quite reach. Then the world went black.

Gradually, I became aware of the young man—*my brother*—trying to revive me, calling out, "Are you okay?" His dark eyes peered into mine. I waved him away and tried to prop myself up on one arm. My head still felt heavy. I scooted across the floor until I could lean my head against the back wall. Anita offered me a cold bottle of water from the case.

Anita took my hand, squeezed it. "Just think how happy your uncle will be! The answer to all his prayers! First his niece comes to visit, then his long-lost son finds him. After all these years."

I gulped the water, trying not to feel anything, trying to let calm and quiet wash over me. I practiced breathing and counting.

"Her uncle?" the young man said. "She's part of the family?"

"That's right, sweetheart. She's your cousin Nea."

The young man stared at me hard. "Nea? I don't remember any Nea. I don't know who this is." He seemed genuinely alarmed.

"It's okay," I said. "I don't remember you either. And Nea wasn't my name before the war. They changed my name in the work camp. They called me Neary, gentle girl. I go by Nea in America. It's easier."

Then the young man smiled. "Ah! Then you must be . . . Sourdi."

The name struck like a fist in my gut. "You remember Sourdi?"

"Of course! My little cousin. You used to come to our house for the new year celebration. I pulled your hair once and made you cry."

"Then the servants were punished instead of you," I said, recalling a story that Sourdi had told me once.

He laughed, delighted.

"Sourdi's my sister," I said quickly. I was lying the way I'd been lied to, but I didn't know what else to say. Once the lie was out, I felt relief. Maybe it was better to be the forgotten cousin. I wasn't sure I wanted to be this person's sister. I wasn't sure I liked him. I didn't trust him. He hadn't been part of any of my reunion plans.

"Does Sourdi work here, too?" He seemed nervous, licking his chapped lips again.

"No, she's married now. She lives in another state far away."

He nodded, relieved, which made me think he had something to hide.

"I'm sorry I don't remember you either, Ponleu."

"It's okay, Nea," he said. "And you call me Paul. I'm more used to that name." He smiled as though genuinely pleased. Relieved again.

Anita decided "the happy reunion" necessitated closing the donut shop so that she could find Uncle. She said Paul and I could get "reacquainted" while she was gone. "But there are going to be a lot of customers, I bet," I said. "And I can man the register."

"Don't even think about it," Anita said. "I know your uncle would want you to get reacquainted with your cousin. Some things are more important than business."

I thought, That is exactly why this business hasn't been doing very well till I got here, but I didn't say it.

Before she left, Anita set out a baguette and a large root beer. "For you, Paul. Have a bite while you're waiting."

He sat in the booth and wolfed down the baguette, taking enormous bites, practically swallowing without chewing. Then he gulped down the soda and chewed the ice.

I got up from the floor and dusted off my jeans. "Would you like a donut?" I asked. I still recognized genuine hunger when I saw it.

"Yes, please," he said. After I gave him three on a napkin, he said, "Thank you, cousin."

He had nice manners, I granted him that.

"I won't ask you any questions, Paul," I said. "I'll let you tell Uncle everything. He's been looking for you for so long."

He nodded and started eating the first donut. He ate methodically, starting at one edge, then munching steadily until it was gone. Then he ate the second, and the third. "They taste like . . ."

"What?"

"Like food I had a long time ago. When I was a boy. Like *you tiao*."

I filled his glass with more root beer and brought it back to him. He thanked me and drained it again quickly.

His hunger seemed intimate. Watching him eat, I felt as though I were violating his privacy. I forced myself to look away, out the window into the parking lot, where the bright California sunlight bleached the cars and the pavement into the same steely shade of gray. A minivan pulled up to the curb, and a woman jumped out and ran to the door. She tried opening it before she noticed the "Closed" sign and returned to her van and drove away.

"Looks like business is good," Paul said.

"It's starting to pick up."

"How much you pull in here a day?" he asked.

That startled me. "Why? Looking for a job?"

He glanced away, his eyes scanning the shops around the strip mall, the grocery, the tanning salon, the copy shop. He squinted, and I wondered if he was disappointed to find his father wasn't the rich man he remembered, or if he'd even figured that out yet.

"So you live around here?" he asked.

"No. I go to school in Nebraska."

"Nebraska," he repeated as he might an unfashionable brand of sneakers, like something that sounded vaguely familiar but undesirable.

We fell into a silence. More customers drove up and then, disappointed, drove away. Finally, the phone rang and I jumped up. It was Anita. She said she'd found Uncle—he'd been translating for a family at the elementary school, but he was coming back right now.

I turned to the young man. "Good news. She found him. They're coming soon."

Paul nodded. Then he stood up and began to pace in a tight circle between the door and the refrigerated case, mouthing something I couldn't make out. Maybe he was saying his prayers, or maybe he was rehearsing his story. I couldn't tell and it didn't seem my place to ask him. Sweat collected on his wide, tan forehead. A vein throbbed at his temple. He patted at his hair, adjusted his shirt. His nervousness was real. He began to look less like a gang member and more like a lost boy, a missing son.

Finally I recognized Uncle's Toyota pulling into the parking lot. "He's here," I said.

Paul froze, standing at attention. He stared out the glass door, watching as Uncle stepped out of his car and made his way across the lot. He opened and shut his mouth without saying anything.

Uncle rushed in the front door, his eyes wide. He stood before Paul. I scanned their faces. Both men looked startled, as though they had caught their reflections in a fun-house mirror and weren't sure what they were looking at.

Paul stepped forward, standing before Uncle, then stopped, suddenly panicking, and searched his pockets frantically. He unfolded the newspaper clipping and held it out to Uncle as though Uncle might not have seen it. "I saw this picture. I recognized you. They don't have your real name, but I knew it was you." He stopped. He swallowed and straightened his shoulders. He ran a hand over his hair. Then he said quickly, reciting from memory the same speech he'd said before, "I am looking for my father. His Khmer name is Chhouen Suoheng. I am the oldest son, Chhouen Ponleu."

Uncle let out a low moan.

"He married my mother, Chhang Sopheam, in Phnom Penh—."

Uncle's mouth dropped open as though he were going to howl, or maybe as though he were already howling silently. His eyes filled with tears. He stepped forward and grabbed Paul, clutched him to his chest. "My son! My son! It's you!"

Paul closed his eyes and held Uncle's shoulders.

Uncle was crying openly now. "Your mother—all these years she looked for you. She refused to give up. She wrote to the Red Cross. She wrote to Refugee Services. She wrote to churches and schools. We drove up and down the state . . ."

Uncle couldn't continue. His mouth opened and closed, but no sound came out.

Paul's face crumpled like a child's, folded in upon itself as though he were made of paper. He folded his broad shoulders inward and put his arm up around the side of his head, a child's gesture, as though he could make himself suddenly invisible, as though he could hide himself from all our eyes while we stared at him and watched him cry.

Then, at last, I had to turn away. It felt obscene to be watching a scene so intimate. To see two men crying, their tears running down their faces. I fell against the counter top, hid my face on my arm, and cried despite myself, felt the hot tears pouring from my eyes against my skin. I should have been happy,

I should have been relieved, but I suddenly felt overwhelming grief that Auntie had not lived to see this moment, this homecoming. It would have meant the world to her. A sign that some god had finally taken pity on her after all her suffering. Surely it would have been enough to keep her alive. But this homecoming had come too late.

CHAPTER 12

In the Days of the White Crocodile

Uncle insisted we close up the shop immediately. He said we should celebrate, although we were all crying. I washed my face in the bathroom sink and tried to smooth down my hair. We drove over to a Chinese restaurant that Uncle liked, where he said he knew the owners, and when we walked in, the waitress stared and turned, then stared again. I knew we all looked like we'd just been in some kind of car wreck. Anita and I were in our work clothes, I had flour on my T-shirt, Anita's nose was red from blowing it, and Uncle and Paul's eyes were swollen. Uncle was smiling now, but in an eerie, detached kind of way, as though he'd just walked out of a rollover and was in shock, surprised to be alive and able to move all his limbs.

It was an old-fashioned diner. The menu still offered chop suey and egg foo young, as well as hamburgers and something called "Oriental Fries."

"This place is a dinosaur," Anita said, "Only the old-timers come around anymore. And they're one of the few places that still allow smoking." She pulled out her pack.

I wasn't hungry, but it didn't matter. We weren't here for the food, but to have someplace to celebrate, though I didn't feel like celebrating either. I felt numb.

Uncle smiled and ordered for everyone, picking dishes as though choosing from an elaborate banquet menu.

As we waited for the food, Uncle gradually grew more animated, as though he were awakening from a long sleep. He beamed and touched Paul's arm as though to make sure he was solid, not a dream. They spoke rapidly in Khmer, too fast for me to join in, describing things I couldn't imagine.

"Do you remember the Chinese restaurant we used to go to when you were young?"

"Every Sunday we had a banquet. I never knew how many people you'd invite—"

"You always had a friend or two from school." Uncle laughed.

"We had fresh steamed crab, stir-fried eels with black-bean sauce, clay-pot chicken with fungus. The rice was so soft and white, like pearls. And you always ordered a fish. You'd fight with your friends, turning it back and forth—"

"The head must point to the most honored guest—"

"You plucked the eyes out with your chopsticks and gave them away. It was a sign of respect, giving away the best parts of the fish."

"What a good memory you have! I'd forgotten that."

"After dinner on the drive home, you once took me and my friends to a French café just to have ice cream. Chocolate. With a long, round, crisp biscuit with a hole in the center."

"You can remember all that?" Uncle was delighted. At last, someone to share his nostalgia, someone who could remember the prosperous life he'd left behind and lost forever.

"But I don't remember my cousin." Paul pointed his chin at me. "I don't remember your real name," he said to me, unapologetically. "But I couldn't believe my eyes when I saw you. You look like my mother."

Uncle shook his head then, hard. He wiped his hands over his eyes. "I have something to tell you."

I waited. My whole body tense. The smells from the kitchen too strong, too oily, making me want to choke. Anita's cigarette smoke curdled in the air around us. The hairs on my arms stood up, the skin on the back of my neck goosepimpled.

"Your mother was waiting for you. She was very ill, but she was trying to stay alive for you. She wanted to see you again so very much."

Paul nodded, listening intensely.

"She tried to find you everywhere. But no use. The Red Cross couldn't find you, we didn't know where you might be. She was very brave, but she'd been injured in a minefield. Some of her wounds never healed." Uncle's voice cracked, and he looked away, wiping his eyes, and we all pretended he wasn't crying in front of us. "I made sure she was buried properly. She no longer believed in such things, but I paid monks to pray for her soul. I paid for the temple to hold the ceremony to guide her soul to the other side. I didn't want people to think I did not respect my wife." Uncle bowed his head and looked away. "If I had known what Pol Pot was planning, if I had known that leaving would cause my family harm, I would not have left you. But after Lon Nol took over, everyone grew paranoid. There was a civil war in the country. You were too young to know about this, but I was accused of being a spy. I didn't even know who I was supposed to be spying for. Some people said I was a spy for Sihanouk. Some people said I was a spy for the CIA. A man came to the house and threatened to do something terrible if I didn't turn myself in. In the beginning, I thought it was ridiculous. Just empty threats to intimidate me.

"One day some of Lon Nol's soldiers came to the house and put a gun to my head. Your mother was very brave. She shouted at the soldiers, 'Go ahead! Shoot him! If he's a spy, I want nothing to do with him!' And they let me go. Maybe it was only a game to intimidate me. Maybe they only wanted money. But other men were killed that day. Colleagues. Everyone was very paranoid. There were real spies in the government, some for the CIA, some for Sihanouk, some for the Vietnamese, maybe even some for Pol Pot. No one knew whom to trust. Even our allies, the Americans, had bombed us. Fourteen months under Sihanouk. Maybe you remember the refugees from the villages pouring into Phnom Penh. Shanty towns sprang up. There were beggars, children and women, so poor and pitiful. Gangs of thieves roamed the streets. Soldiers from rival factions hid among the survivors and fought each other, throwing hand grenades at cyclo drivers, into theaters, in front of restaurants.

"I tried to keep you safe. I hired a driver to take you to elementary school. It was no longer safe for ordinary people to walk or ride in *tuk-tuk*s or cyclos. Your mother was ill. She couldn't watch you, a growing boy. You were so clever—you didn't want to stay inside all day. You found ways to escape the house. I used to beat you, I was so afraid you'd be hurt, but it was no use. What does a little boy know?

"When the Americans' ally, Lon Nol, overthrew Sihanouk and proclaimed himself head of state, we thought the bombings would stop. Lon Nol was Sino-Khmer. He reached out to the Chinese business community. He said he wanted to stop the war, make Cambodia strong and prosperous again. That's why I agreed to work for him. I didn't like him, but we were all looking for a solution. But the American bombings didn't stop. The Americans sent ground troops. Lon Nol did not object. We thought he must be mad. But what did he know? The Americans were fighting the Communists in Vietnam, but they accused Cambodia of harboring the Viet Cong. They bombed the border, trying to keep the Vietnamese out. The Americans sent troops into the mountains. But the Communists were strong, too. The Soviet Union and China gave them weapons and money. The Americans said Lon Nol was corrupt. He took their aid money and didn't pay his troops. It's true. He didn't. But we were a small country, and we were like grass trapped beneath warring elephants.

"After the soldiers came to the house and threatened to shoot me in front of your mother, I realized I was putting the whole family in danger. If I didn't leave, they would come again and again. What if they shot the children? I thought. Your mother agreed. I would leave, and she would denounce me publicly as a coward who had abandoned the family. Then, after I had established myself abroad, I would send for you all. Your youngest brother was only a year old. We didn't think it was safe for the family to travel. Not with so young an infant. I thought it would be safer for your mother to stay in Phnom Penh. Her family could help her with the children. I would leave all the money with her. I figured no matter how bad things got in the countryside, Phnom Penh would be safe. The Americans would not let the capital fall. That's how we all thought in those days.

"First I went to Malaysia and worked for a Chinese businessman. My father's family had made its fortune in the pepper trade, and I thought I could be a liaison for him with foreign trading companies that we had worked with. I went in the fall of 1974 and tried to establish myself in business. I sent letters to your mother. Not directly, in case she was being watched. But I sent them to friends to let her know I was okay, and that I would call for her soon. She wrote to me, sending the letters through a third party. But then, in April 1975, when the Khmer Rouge took the capital, suddenly there was no word from Phnom Penh. It was like the whole country had disappeared off the earth. I could not send a telegram. I could not call. I could not reach your mother. From the few accounts from Western journalists still in the capital, I knew something terrible was happening. I tried to buy a ticket to return immediately, but I could not find a flight going in. Then my bank accounts were frozen. I had no money. I wrote to friends in Thailand, in Hong Kong, but no one knew how to reach you.

"When it became clear to the world that something had gone terribly wrong in Cambodia, I was able to come as a refugee to America. I still had some business ties. But for four years, I heard nothing. I could not find my family. I could not find you. Then, after the Vietnamese Army invaded in 1978, more information began to pour out into the world. I found your mother through the Red Cross. I was living in Texas by this time. I was able to sponsor her to America. But it was too late! She told me what she had had to endure. She told me how she had to watch our children die.

"She should have hated me. She should have blamed me. What kind of man am I? A man who cannot protect his family! A man who leaves his family! But she blamed herself!"

Uncle was crying without tears. His face was contorted by grief, a mask of his former face. His body shook and he put his hands in front of his eyes.

Anita touched his arm, and eventually his breathing steadied.

"I wish I could have seen *Mai* again," Paul said simply. His voice was quiet, seemingly calm, but I could see the veins on his neck throbbing from the beat of his heart.

The food on the table congealed on the platters around us. None of us had any appetite at all.

After Uncle regained his composure and was able to drink a full cup of hot tea, Paul decided to tell us a story. I thought he'd start with how he came to be in America, his sponsors, how he'd been living all these years, but no, he wanted to tell us about something he remembered from back when he was a rich kid with too much time on his hands.

"Do you remember I captured a baby white crocodile? Everyone was talking about the ghost crocodile in those days. It was a bad sign, a magic beast. The servants were so afraid, but you told them not to worry. It was just a superstition, just a story. It couldn't really hurt us."

"I'd forgotten. You caught something. Some kind of animal. Your mother was upset about some animal. I don't remember."

"It was a baby white crocodile. Just like the story," Paul insisted.

He described how he and his friends had overheard the servants talking about the rumors of this giant beast swimming into the city via the Mekong, escaping the river and climbing the banks near a rubber factory. It was living in the slums around Phnom Penh, hiding in the shanties that had sprung up after the peasants started moving from the countryside, trying to escape the Americans' bombing raids on the northeastern border. Entire villages were being built from the bits and pieces of garbage that the city people had thrown away, the scraps of tin and the bricks they could steal here and there. The boys had been warned to stay away from the shanties; it was dangerous, there were soldiers hiding there, spies, thieves. But my brother had heard about the crocodile and now he wanted to see for himself.

The white crocodile had appeared in Phnom Penh in the first year after the fall of the old government, after it became clear that Prince Sihanouk would not return. Workers spotted it lurking in the shallows of the Mekong where factory effluent poured directly into the muddy water. Then refugees from bombed-out villages swore they'd seen it crawling in the shadowy overgrown alleyways where they sold fruit. The rumors grew more urgent: *The white crocodile is hungry. It eats small children and dogs. Teach your children to run, fast.* Every missing person became a sign that the crocodile was near. The police stayed clear, but a group of soldiers came and shot up a farmer's fruit stand, saying the smell of rotting papaya in the sunlight was attracting the beast. The rumors continued, spreading like a summer influenza from the shanties to the street markets to the schools and temples and churches. At the cathedral, a priest offered up a Mass and the penance of his parishioners if God would remove the monstrosity. Monks and their novices chanted through the night: the white crocodile has returned, the world is ending, a new world is dawning. Over and over, their prayers drifted on the wind, thick as incense. It was hard to tell if the monks were mourning or rejoicing.

My brother was different. For him, the white crocodile was an opportunity.

He was still in primary school, maybe eight, nine years old, when he convinced his friends that they should not only skip class to look for the white crocodile, but that they should also capture it. He'd even thought of where to put it—in the court-yard pond of his best friend Arun's house.

"Your yard is the biggest. You have a fish pond." My brother ticked off its crocodile-worthy attributes on his long, tan fingers. "Plus, now that your father has broken his leg, he won't think to look in the back. And the servants are too busy to bother with the yard."

Arun's lips quivered. He picked at his nose as though there were a direct pathway to his brain that could be tapped if he only dug deep enough. "I don't know. My mother will get angry at me."

"Your mother!" My brother laughed. "Ha ha. Arun's afraid of his mother!"

The other boys laughed, uncertain. They were young, after all. They were all in fact afraid of their own mothers. They were not sure how to turn on a friend and make something ordinary seem like a moral flaw. Soon they would, but not quite yet.

My brother was ahead of his time.

The next morning all four of the boys went to school as usual under the watchful eyes of their family servants. They waved politely from the school yard, waiting for their escorts to turn the corner and disappear from sight. Then one by one, the four boys ran back through the school's front gate and down the broad street, meeting under the flame tree across from the fried-cricket stand as planned.

My brother commandeered a *tuk-tuk* to take them to the slums, where their families would never let them go. They clambered into the back seat of the brightly painted wooden cart attached to the small moped. The driver was a teenager, barely out of boyhood himself, but he confidently headed into the crowded streets, steering around oxcarts and bicycle-powered cyclos. The boys were thrilled to be out of school and in the thick of the city. They waved cheerily at the honking Renault 2CVs and the occasional black Mercedes that sped past them. The *tuk-tuk* wove around garbage and potholes and bands of street children coming to beg. No matter how bad the terrain, the young *tuk-tuk* driver could navigate without tipping over.

That's when my brother realized how useful this teenager might be. When they finally stopped at the edge of a row of shacks where the dirt road ended at the river's bank, my brother invited their driver along. "Come with us and we'll buy you something to eat." The boy, fresh from a village, had no reason not to trust them, my brother said.

Together, my brother, his friends, and the *tuk-tuk* driver walked to the bank of the river. There they saw many dead and discarded things: bloated fish, drowned lizards, a shoe, a man's leg. And then, in the shallows, insects buzzing around its yellow eyes, was a baby crocodile, already more than a foot long. It appeared lost, too young to be away from its mother. It looked emaciated, pale, sick. Not dark like ordinary crocodiles, but chalk-colored. The boys approached, and the crocodile startled. It tried to head to deeper water, but it was caught. It thrashed about, its hind leg trapped in a plastic soda ring, the kind that arrived with the Americans, holding their cans of Coca-Cola together. Trash thrown into the river had trapped the baby crocodile on the bank and kept it from returning to its mother, and now it lay dying in the hot sun.

My brother told the *tuk-tuk* driver to go pick it up. "I'll buy you ice cream when we get back to the city," he said.

"What's ice cream?" the driver asked.

"The best food in the world," my brother said.

"I want rice soup noodles," the driver said, bargaining. "I want an egg."

"Fine, a bowl of soup noodles with an egg in it, but you have to go down there and pick up that crocodile and bring it back to us."

The driver looked at the creature dying in the dried mud.

"I'll buy a whole bowl of noodle soup just for you."

"With an egg," the driver said.

"I promise. With an egg."

The driver smiled widely, believing he'd gotten the better end of the bargain, and scampered down among the detritus along the riverbank. He pushed through the thick reeds and edged past the garbage, the rotting human leg, and the leather shoe, until finally he was standing on the dried mud. He was leaning over to pick up the crocodile when the creature whipped its tail once and bit the teenager on the finger.

"Ow!" he cried out, loudly.

"You're okay. You're bigger than he is. He can't hurt you," my brother coached, from the safety of the road. "Go on, grab him. Just hold his mouth together with your hands and pull him up."

The driver looked unsure. He held his bleeding finger in the air.

"I can see your finger. You're fine. It's not a big bite. Just be fast this time. Come on! Do you want your soup noodles or not?"

The teenager wiped his bleeding finger on the back of his *sampot* and charged at the crocodile. He kept his hands outstretched and danced around the crocodile, which flipped its tail feebly and made a second, halfhearted lunge at the driver. This time the teenager was prepared. He grabbed the crocodile's neck with one hand and clamped the other around its mouth. Then he pulled the creature from the earth and ran back up the riverbank toward the road, smiling broadly.

"Good job!" my brother said. "Now we need something to carry it in." He ordered one of his friends to empty his school satchel to hold the crocodile. "Wait. Don't let go of it yet," my brother commanded the driver. He uprooted a reed from the side of the road and wrapped it around the crocodile's snout. "There," he said, satisfied, and they stuffed the beast into the book bag.

They climbed back into the *tuk-tuk*, setting the thrashing satchel on the seat of the moped, and the driver, standing balanced on the pedals, drove them back into the city.

But when they paused at an intersection, waiting for an elephant to pass, a police officer spotted the crocodile's tail poking out of the bag and ordered the driver to stop. "What have you boys got there? Come here!"

My brother grabbed the satchel with the crocodile, and he and Arun took off in one direction, his two classmates in the other. The police officer decided to cut his losses and grabbed the driver, pulling him off his moped.

From a hiding place behind a stand where a woman sold drinks from a bucket, my brother watched as the police officer dragged the teenager off and another officer confiscated the vehicle.

My brother said he felt bad the driver had been caught, but he figured there was nothing he could do. He didn't want to get caught himself and be forced to give up the crocodile.

So he and Arun waited until the cops disappeared and then hired a cyclo driver to take them back home.

While the servants were busy, the boys dumped the crocodile in the fishpond in the courtyard garden of Arun's house, but the beast was listless. It floated to the side of the pond and stayed there, refusing to wreak havoc among the goldfish as they'd hoped.

The next morning the baby crocodile was dead. The gardener found it floating on the surface of the pond, belly up. Arun's mother called to complain, but my brother said our mother didn't have the heart to punish him. He said he was lucky our father never found out about the escapade.

The servants would gossip for months afterward. How had the crocodile gotten into the yard? Where had it come from? And what had given it such a ghostly color?

"I used to wonder if I'd caused it all," my brother said. "If everyone was right about the white crocodile. If I'd caused all the bad things to happen."

"You were just a boy," Uncle said. "And it's just a superstition."

"I know," said my brother. "But that's how I thought."

Uncle looked away, as though he felt even guiltier than he had before.

"I wonder what happened to the *tuk-tuk* driver," I said, at the end of the story. "Did you ever see him again?"

"Him? Ha. That kind of person was king under Pol Pot. That kind of boy had it easy." Then he laughed a bitter *ha ha ha*, which made me realize how much anger he held inside his bones.

PART FIVE

Don't keep a thin tiger as a pet.
—traditional Cambodian proverb

CHAPTER 13

The View from the Aquarium

Back at the apartment, I could tell Paul was disappointed. He looked around at the bare walls, the spartan furnishings, the small kitchen, and I knew he was weighing the present against the heft of his memories: the three-story home, the courtyard, the servants. He stood in the very center of the living room, in front of the couch that was now my bed, looking this way and that, pigeonlike, as though his eyes couldn't quite focus on the smallness of the place, as though he thought that if he found just the right angle he'd discover the magic portal that opened up to the penthouse he'd been longing for.

"How many buildings does he own?" he asked me while Uncle rummaged in the closet.

I shrugged, because it seemed better than saying, "None."

Paul paced back and forth from the door to the window, looking down upon the crabgrass lawn, the parking lot, the street. He could bound across the width of the apartment in three large steps. He paused at the window, squinting into the sun.

Uncle brought out clean sheets, blankets. "I'm sorry you'll have to sleep on the floor until I can buy you a mattress."

Paul smiled politely. "Thank you."

Then they sat down at the kitchen table while I boiled water for tea. Uncle seemed dazed. I imagined that a deer that had been struck by a moving vehicle might stagger off a road with the same look that Uncle had on his face.

Over cups of black tea, Uncle asked about Paul's life now. Paul said he'd been working in L.A., nothing special, just jobs to get by. He'd escaped to a refugee camp in Thailand when he was fourteen. As an unaccompanied minor, he'd been put with another family in the camp, and they had been sponsored to come to America as a group. All his papers filed with the Red Cross and the INS and his schools had this family's name on it. After he got to America, he didn't dare tell anyone that that wasn't his name. The family said that if the government found out they'd lied, he'd be sent back to Cambodia or forced to fend for himself in the refugee camp. Then when he got older, the family said he owed them for taking care of him, and made him pay them back, made him work for them for free. He didn't want to be their slave, so he ran away at seventeen. He'd been working ever since. This and that, any odd job he could find to get by, since he hadn't been able to go on with school. He still remembered what he'd learned in Chinese school in Phnom Penh, so he was able to get work in Chinatown, first as a stock boy, then as a waiter. Sometimes he'd helped a bookie collect on debts. That was when he'd learned to dress tough. A lot of violence could be avoided just through intimidation. He'd done some landscaping, construction. He'd tried to put some money aside to start his own business someday.

Uncle nodded. "You can live with me. You can work with me."

"How many donut shops do you have? How many apartments?"

He was disappointed to learn Uncle had only one of each.

I knew he was going to be even more disappointed to learn that Uncle was no longer rich and donated away his pastries to the church and to all his volunteer projects.

"I remember our house," Paul said softly, shaking his head. "I remember our Mercedes. I remember you wore a suit, with a tie, and leather shoes to go to work."

Uncle looked at the kitchen tabletop, pushed his teacup from one hand to the other.

"I used to think it was my fault," Paul said. "Everything. When I was a kid, I thought I was to blame."

He laughed in a rueful, ironic way. And I wondered if his memories of wealth had sustained him during the Pol Pot years, in the refugee camp, in America, this hope that someday he'd find his rich father and everything would be returned to him. I couldn't tell just by looking at him what he thought now. The light from the setting sun fell thick and gold against his skin, coating him in a honey glow that softened the hard edges of his jaw, smoothed the rough angles of his broken nose. Looking at him, I tried to see something of Uncle's face in his, but could not. I excused myself and went to the bathroom, just so that I could stare at my own face in the mirror, see if I recognized my brother's features in my own, but my complexion was fair—washed-out to my eyes—and round-faced, the kind of blurry face that made me look younger and less mature in my professors' eyes. I possessed none of the angles present on the faces of fashion models in magazines. My brother had those edges, had that chiseled look. I realized he was probably considered quite handsome.

Had Uncle looked like this when he was younger? I wondered. Paul didn't look like Sitan, whose face was wide and sweet, Buddha-like, with his fleshy soft lips, wide nose, long earlobes. Sitan had the kind face of someone born in a gentler time. Paul, on the other hand, actually looked like someone who had survived a war, like someone who'd seen a lot of people die. He looked like someone who still knew how to fight. Like someone who might start a fight, too, and win it.

Staring at the mirror, I decided only my eyes looked like Paul's. They held the same flashes of anger, had the same habit of looking out of the corners to see what was sneaking up on us, but I had no way to know if that was genetic, or simply the habit of someone with a suspicious nature.

For the first time since my arrival, Uncle had not gone to work overnight supervising the bakers. Instead he listened all night as Paul told crazy story after crazy story about life before Pol Pot, all his wonderful memories of the movies he'd seen, the meals he'd eaten in fancy restaurants, the pranks he'd played with his friends. Uncle nodded and smiled, as though the past were a book they could share, pass back and forth, reciting their favorite passages.

Paul didn't get up for breakfast, just grumbled from his blankets on the floor when I said it was time to leave for work. Uncle said we shouldn't disturb him. Even though I hadn't slept at all, between listening to Paul's stories and then his snores, I didn't say anything. I went with Uncle to the donut shop as usual, and I was pleased that we still had a rush of new customers show up, enticed by the article, willing to drive out of their way to try a taste of Little Phnom Penh, as the reporter had dubbed it.

Sitan came in early, excited by the gossip about Uncle's long-lost son turning up.

"It's a dream come true," Anita told Sitan. "That poor man. What he and his wife went through all those years."

"Karma," Sitan said emphatically. "For doing all those good things he does."

"I thought you had to wait for your next life for karma to kick in," I said.

They ignored my cynicism.

Paul showed up mid-afternoon, sauntering in the front door, mirrored sunglasses on his nose. He didn't offer to help, but stood back and watched us work. Finally when there was a lull, he stepped up the counter and tapped the register.

"How much this place bring in per week?"

I shook my head. "I don't know. But we just launched the public relations campaign to increase business two weeks ago."

He laughed in my face. "Come on, how much business you think a place like this can do? In the city, I know people who pull ten thousand a week cash with a coffee stand. This place wouldn't make that in a month, maybe three. You can't run a business in the sticks."

I wanted to tell him to go back to the people he knew in the city and work for them again if he liked it so much. I wanted to ask why, if he had all these rich friends, he was living out of his car. But I kept my mouth closed, tightly. It was too soon to pick a fight, what with everyone so excited to see the long-lost son return.

Anita tacked diplomatic. "Well, sugar, if you've got a business plan, I'm sure your father would be interested in talking it over with you."

"We should liquidate this place and move. Location is everything. This town is dead."

I stood up straight behind the counter. "Uncle has a small-business loan to retrain Khmer refugees—"

"Yeah, he told me about those two old women who come in. He's thinking too small."

"You don't know them. You didn't even get up till afternoon. They work way harder than you. And they are very talented."

"Listen, college girl, I know how the real world works." He switched to Khmer, speaking rapidly, his face flushing. "My father can do better than this. He is an educated man. He was an important member of the transitional government. He does not have to live like a beggar in this country."

"Who's living like a beggar?" I demanded. "You're the one who came looking for a handout!"

"And what about you? Why are you here?"

"Well, sounds like you two are having quite the discussion." Anita swept between us, smiling brightly, carrying two glasses of iced tea. "How about a little tea to cool off?"

Anita sat with Paul in the booth, sipping tea and pretending to be interested in Paul's "business plan," as she called it. "You could be a real boon to your father," I heard her say.

I turned to Sitan as I furiously wiped the counter. "I can't believe she's humoring him. It's like he's got some kind of Tourette's syndrome. He's so rude! Comes here and disses the donut shop just as we're taking off."

Sitan laughed. "He's just like you. You did the same thing."

"We're nothing alike!"

"First thing you did after you got here was try to change the business. You said it was failing. You made all those coupons. You wrote that reporter. Maybe Paul will come up with a good idea, too." Sitan winked at me. "Yo, maybe it runs in the family."

I didn't answer. Instead I decided it was time to take the trash out. No point wasting my energy listening to such nonsense.

At sunset when Uncle returned to close up, Paul surprised me with a request. "How about I take Sitan and Nea with me for a night out?"

I thought Uncle would be disappointed, expect Paul to want to spend more time with him, but Paul continued obliviously, "I have some friends who work at a club outside San Bernardino. I'll drive everyone."

Uncle nodded. "It will be good for you all to get to know each other." He seemed disappointed and hopeful at the same time, and I realized he wanted us to get along.

"You'll like this place," Paul told Sitan. "Got the best beats."

"I don't want to go to some skanky strip club," I said.

"Not that kind of club. I have good taste."

I rolled my eyes.

"You bring any nice clothes with you?" He appraised my jeans and sweatshirt. "Don't worry. I know the bouncer. I'll put in a word for you."

So I found myself crammed in the back seat of Paul's Mazda, my knees pressed against the back of Sitan's seat while Paul and Sitan laughed, the music on the stereo so loud I felt it in my bones.

Paul drove fast, weaving in and out of traffic. He liked to come up right behind a car and hover on its bumper before darting around it. Then he raced to tailgate the next car. I knew this said something profound about insecurity and his ego, but for the time being it made me worry about the front of the car smashing into metal and the car folding like pleats against my flesh and bones.

"Take it easy," I piped up from the back seat. "I don't want to get in an accident." My voice sounded thin to my own ears.

"Of course," Paul said, then laughed and sped up.

This continued for a half hour.

The club he eventually took us to wasn't as divey as I'd feared, not like the places I'd seen in movies, where you expect a large, uncontrolled fire to break out and burn everyone alive, but it wasn't fancy either, with an actual velvet rope and a line of eager patrons begging to be let in while movie star wannabes and models sashayed through the door. It was situated in a nondescript part of some town I'd never heard of, the paint fading, a neon sign flashing in the window, and a group of giggly girls and their dates showing IDs to get inside. The bouncer looked more bored than intimidating, just a large brown man seated on a stool, waiting for the time to pass.

I expected Paul to be in his element, but he seemed nervous as we walked up to the door. He hung back as he waited for a group of loud friends to laugh their way inside, then he slunk up to the bouncer.

"Yo, bro, whazzup."

The bouncer looked mildly surprised. "I didn't expect to see you."

"I brought family." Paul smiled and nodded at Sitan and me.

"That so?"

"Seriously, can you let us in?"

The bouncer looked left and right. "Donny's not working tonight, but if you see Bill, I'm not responsible."

"It's okay. I got a new job."

"Your funeral." He let us pass, then at the last second, the bouncer grabbed my wrist. "Wait a sec, you got any ID?"

I pulled out my student ID, and he stamped each of my hands with a large X.

"Be good," he said.

I couldn't think of any super-smart retort, so I just nodded like a dork. Then I realized Paul and Sitan had gone on without me. I hurried after them. At college I'd gone to dances near campus and one held in the gymnasium. I wasn't sure what to expect in a real California club. I'd seen movies and crime shows on TV. Maybe I expected movie stars and dead bodies. As I stepped inside, my first impression was that it was too dark and kind of dingy. Large cutouts of exotic aquarium fish adorned the walls, and dusty-looking nets swooped down from the ceiling. The bar had weird spotlights on it, which reflected off the mirrors along the wall and created blinding hot spots. The music wasn't bad, but it was a little dated; a remix of George Michael's "I Want Your Sex" boomed from the speakers. The beat was danceable, but the floor was mostly deserted. A couple of girls wearing an entire drugstore's worth of Revlon were flipping their long, curly hair over alternate shoulders. I couldn't see the faces of the men who were inspiring the hair-flipping, but they were dressed in ill-fitting suits, as though they'd stopped in to drink after a long day of selling insurance or used cars. I was disappointed. My first time in a California club and it wasn't as good as the clubs that catered to the drunken frat boys and sodden sorority girls at school, the kind of places that used black lights so everyone's teeth glowed in the dark.

Paul didn't seem interested in dancing. He stood at the bar, holding a beer without drinking, as he talked to the bartender, asking him about business, meaningless small talk, as far as I could hear. Sitan nursed a Dos Equis as he surveyed the dance floor, bobbing his head.

A group of the most beautiful girls I'd ever seen danced in a circle, but most of the men just stood around the edge of the dance floor, carrying their drinks, watching.

"This place is lame!" I said. "A total meat market."

Sitan shrugged. "I wouldn't have gone to a place like this back in the day, I was really prejudiced. But I'm better now. I'm learning to be more tolerant."

"You wouldn't have wanted a gig here? Too small?" I asked.

He laughed. "Good one, Nea!" He patted me on the shoulder.

While I nursed a Diet Coke, Paul got into an earnest-looking discussion with a stocky Asian girl with dyed red hair and enough makeup to make Ronald McDonald blush. The conversation didn't seem to go over very well. Paul grew more and more agitated, waving his arms through the air, then folding them over his chest, then holding his hands out like a supplicant. He smiled, showing all his teeth, like a monkey trying to curry favor with a king. The woman seemed singularly unimpressed, and when she turned to go, Paul jumped off the barstool and stood before her, before she pushed past and disappeared into a circle of friends on the fringes of the dance floor.

Sitan disappeared briefly, then popped up on the floor, dancing to Madonna's "Vogue."

Finally Paul reappeared at my elbow, his mouth a straight line, his brow furrowed.

"What's the matter?"

He shook his head. "We should get out. Nothing going on."

We waded into the drinkers till we found Sitan trading moves with a bulky-looking girl with bleached-blond hair and tattoos of tears dripping down her left cheek.

Paul pulled him loose and we headed outside.

"You got some moves on you," I told Sitan, who smiled shyly as we walked out into the parking lot. The air was cold and I pulled my jacket around my body. The sky was black and far away, the stars little pinpricks of ice.

"I wouldn't have thought it, but those drag queens can really dance."

"Drag queens!" I glanced back over my shoulder.

"What, you couldn't tell?" Sitan laughed at me. "You really are from Nebraska."

I felt my cheeks burning hot. "I knew," I lied. "But not all the girls were in drag, right?"

Sitan shook his head. "Fresh off the farm," he snickered.

Suddenly, there was a flash of two headlights headed straight our way. A man's voice boomed, "What the hell you doing back here?"

"Shit, my old boss." Paul shook his head. "We're leaving!" he called over his shoulder as he ushered us toward his car.

But the man jumped out and ran up to Paul, grabbing him by the collar of his leather jacket. "I thought I told you I never wanted to see you around here again!" He shoved Paul hard.

"Hey, that's assault. You can't do that," I said.

"Who says I can't?"

"ACLU. This is a public space. We were peaceably assembled. Now we're going back to our car. You can't just physically strike someone. That's assault."

The man stepped into a yellow puddle of light from one of the lights in the parking lot. He was bald and barrel-chested, wearing a suit jacket and a silky shirt open at the neck. I couldn't tell if he was white or a very pale brown man. "What's all this AC-DC IOU shit?"

"It's okay, man, we're leaving, we're leaving. Just my little cousin. She's in college is all. You know how crazy those college girls talk," Sitan stepped between me and the sweaty bald guy.

"You better clear your ass out," he said to Paul. Then he glared at me and actually raised a fist and shook it. "As for you, smart-mouth—"

"You touch me and I'll press charges! I'll call my lawyer! See how you like that! You can't go around hitting people! That's against the law!"

"This is my business, smarty-pants. I can do what I want." The man punched his fist into his palm.

"You touch me, I'll sue you!"

Sitan was dragging me across the parking lot. "Hurry up," he said.

"You could go to jail!" I shouted over my shoulder. "See how you like that!"

Paul hurriedly unlocked the doors of his Mazda, and Sitan pushed me in the front seat, then he scrambled over me, his knees in my face, and landed with a thump in the back seat. Paul hit the gas, and the tires squealed against the asphalt as we tore off down the street toward the highway.

"What's the matter with you?" Paul muttered.

"What's the matter with *me*? What's the matter with your asshole friend? It's totally illegal to threaten to hit people."

Sitan peered out the back window as though he expected cars to come chasing after us.

"So you worked in that club?" I asked, calming down a little. I fastened my seatbelt. "You a bouncer or a bartender?"

"Neither. He was my supplier."

I sat back with a hollow feeling in my gut.

Sitan whistled from the back seat. "Don't go messing with those people."

"I'm clean now. I'm not going back to that life."

"Then why did you go back to that club if you knew your 'dealer' was there?" My heart was pounding in my ears.

"I needed to talk to someone."

"That woman?" Then I corrected myself. "I mean, that guy?"

"No, someone else. Her friend."

I knew I should tell Uncle about all this, the drug dealing, the search for a missing woman in *his old dealer's* club, but part of me worried that Uncle wouldn't want to hear what I would have to say. And bad news could have a way of boomeranging on the messenger. There was a lot of bad news Ma hadn't wanted to hear over the years when I was growing up. Part of me felt weary. Was it still worth fighting the way I had as a child?

Sitan was laughing from the back seat.

"This isn't funny!" I said.

"Shut up! Both of you!" Paul slammed his fist against the dashboard. Then he picked up the speed, tailgating again.

Great, I thought. We were going to get in an accident for sure.

Paul turned on the radio, and we listened to bad, loud pop all the way back to our exit to Santa Bonita.

CHAPTER 14

The Lost Boys

When we got back to the apartment, Uncle was nowhere to be found. There was a note in his spidery cursive anchored to the kitchen table with a grapefruit: "Glad you have a fun time together! This is special Ruby Red. Try it for breakfast."

It seemed early for him to have gone back to the donut shop, but Sitan didn't seem worried. "He stays with friends sometimes," Sitan said. "Back when I needed a place to stay, he used to let me stay here, and he stayed somewhere else."

"What do you mean? What friends? Where?" I asked.

But Sitan shrugged. "Don't worry. It's just the way he is sometimes."

"Have you noticed all the Sudafed he's taking?" I asked, since Sitan seemed to want to be the expert on Uncle. "And the Nicorette? When did he start smoking?"

Sitan shook his head.

"I think there's something wrong. He didn't used to be this way."

"Nothing used to be this way," Paul interjected. He was pacing around the apartment, taking long strides from the kitchenette to the front door, from the bookshelf to the opposite wall, as though he were measuring. "The old world ended. Back to Year Zero. Don't you remember?"

I ignored him. "Sitan, Uncle seems to like you very much. He obviously trusts you. You must have known him for a while. Do you think he's behaving rationally?"

Sitan picked up the grapefruit and tossed it from hand to hand. "You sound like an old woman."

"You sound like a jerk."

Paul stepped between us. "Hey, how about a smoke?" He held up a joint.

"If Uncle comes back, he'll smell it."

He and Sitan smirked, but then decided to go smoke on the fire escape. They slipped out the front door while I rummaged in the refrigerator for something to make for dinner. I turned on the TV, but Uncle didn't get cable and there wasn't much on—a sitcom, a medical drama, an animated Christmas special with singing animals, and an episode of *Cops*. I turned off the TV and ate my leftovers in silence, watching the occasional headlights pull into the parking lot, the shadows of a mulberry tree dance across the far wall, the flicker of shadow and light against the drapes. Life in California wasn't glamorous the way I'd imagined. I could believe it would be a lot like life at home if I stayed—working around the clock in the family business, trying to find time to study if I went to school here—only it would be lonelier. I'd moved so many times, how could I have forgotten this empty feeling of being far from any friends? I realized I hadn't thought out this trip very well at all.

Around midnight, Paul and Sitan returned, smelling of smoke and the pizza they'd ordered and shared.

Sitan grabbed my pillows off the sofa, stretched out on the floor, and fell asleep almost immediately, but Paul continued to pace.

"What's wrong?" I asked.

"I wish *Mai* were still alive," he said. "I always thought she must have died in Cambodia."

I didn't tell him that part of her did, and that the woman who'd made it to America was nothing like the mother he remembered. I said simply, "She missed you."

"Did she say what she thought happened to me? Did she say where she thought the soldiers took me?" His voice was angry.

"Nobody knew where you went. She could only hope you were still alive."

"Ha," he said, and the anger in his voice made me realize he might blame our mother for not taking care of him, for not having protected him. It wasn't rational, but the way he held his face, his features squeezed together now, made me think of a child trying not to cry, not a twenty-five-year-old man thinking about the past.

Then Paul began to tell me his own story, how he and his best friend survived under the Khmer Rouge. We all had such stories, each one different and the same. "If not for him, I would be dead. He was like my brother. We were the only family we had." He spoke in his beautiful Khmer, the grammar perfect, like our mother's, like our father's. I couldn't follow everything he said at first, I wasn't used to the vocabulary, but then as I listened, I found I understood more and more, the language sliding into a corner in my brain that I hadn't known existed.

When he was eleven, the soldiers took my brother from the rest of the family and sent him to a camp for young men. Some of the boys were trained as soldiers, the so-called Old People, the ones who'd grown up in the countryside their whole lives and were considered the most "pure." They were uninfluenced by the city's foreign elements, uneducated, and unable to contradict the Khmer Rouge's new version of Cambodian history. As one of the former City Boys, my brother was one of the New People. He was among those forced to work the hardest, digging drainage ditches for a road the soldiers wanted to build.

Later, the City Boys were sent into the mountains to help build a road. He had to hack through the jungle, clearing brush and vines and earth away in metal buckets on a pole slung over his shoulders. Many of the City Boys grew sick in the jungle, coughing in the cold night air, shivering from fevers, doubling over from the crippling diarrhea. Then, one by one, they died. Sometimes they were criticized for small errors—falling, tripping, dropping a bucket. Often they were beaten by the soldiers for no reason at all. One day several of the Country Boys accused a City Boy of something. It wasn't clear what he'd done wrong. They said he'd complained about the hard work. They said he was only pretending to be injured. But who would dare to complain? Who would dare to malinger? The City Boy and his entire group of friends were led away into the jungle, and my brother never saw them again. He knew from his previous work camp that boys who were led off were generally killed, their bodies left to rot in the sun and feed the large black birds that circled in the sky, thick as the smoke of a funeral pyre.

At night my brother huddled together with his best friend, Arun. They didn't dare talk about the past anymore, their lives as classmates in Phnom Penh. They'd long ago decided on their story. They were war orphans, American bombs had fallen on their villages, their relatives had taken them to the capital's shanty towns to escape, and they'd lived as beggars. They could describe the slums from their experience crocodile hunting. If anyone asked about their accents, they'd shrug. They'd had to learn to speak like City Boys or they couldn't beg for work, for food, for money.

In the first camp, they were lucky. Some of the Country Boys liked to hear them talk about life in the city. What did the buildings look like? What kind of food did the city people eat? Did you ever see the King's palace? Did you see the dancing girls? Were they pretty? How pretty? Some of the Country Boys sat rapt and wide-eyed, listening to the tales of a life they'd only dreamed about before the Khmer Rouge took over. But Paul and Arun had to be careful so that the *chhlops* didn't hear them. Those children trained as spies would have turned them all in to the older men, who'd have killed them for talking about the pre-revolutionary past.

Arun was a good storyteller. He could remember the plot of every movie he'd ever seen. The other boys particularly liked the story of the snake spirit who pretended to be a beautiful woman so that she could marry an unsuspecting farmer. One night the husband followed his wife to a forest lake where she liked to bathe in privacy. He watched from behind a large boulder as she took off her clothes and stepped into the clear water, the moonlight shining like silver against her skin. Mesmerized by her beauty, he had climbed onto the rock so that he could watch her swim, when, in the bright silver light of the moon, he saw her reflection on the surface of the water, shiny as a mirror. He saw the face of a medusa, her hair coiling with snakes. He ran home terrified, unsure what the vision had meant. Nine months later when their first child was born, the little girl emerged with tiny snakes for hair. Horrified, he accused his wife of being a demon, and she slithered away to a cave, never to be seen again.

He remembered the plots of Hong Kong movies with flying Chinese swordsmen spinning through the air as they fought with villains, rescuing entire villages from masked bandits, demons who shot fire out of their hands, and wicked officials who stole from the poor. He could recount the complicated plots of Indian movies with bandits, star-crossed lovers, motorcycles, car chases, dance interludes, and beautiful, red-lipped women who sang in the sweet, high voices of little girls.

Sometimes the village boys would trade a little of their rice rations to hear another movie recounted from beginning to end.

But in the next camp, the work was harder, death felt closer, and the rice was less than a tight fistful for the entire work crew of boys. They filled their stomachs with the dirty water that was served instead of soup. They kept stones in their mouths all day, sucking on them, rolling them against their dry tongues, trying to keep the dreadful feeling of hunger at bay. To show weakness was to ask for death. Dying might not have been so bad, but the soldiers had taken to cutting out the organs of the men and boys they killed, boiling them as soup, drinking the gall of human bladders, sharing the livers of the dying as meat.

At night, he and Arun had smelled the scent of burning flesh on the wind.

"If they come for us," Arun had whispered in the night, while they lay on the hard ground, the sounds of the jungle's beasts carried on the wind, the sound of the others boys' breathing filling the night around them, "if they try to take us away, I'll kill you first."

My brother had been grateful. "If they come for us, we'll run fast, so they'll have to shoot us," he said.

The thought of dying together quickly was a consolation. It was enough to sustain my brother. It helped him to endure, to keep living, knowing that he had such a loyal friend in the whole dark world. Better than a brother.

Their chance for escape came when the Vietnamese army invaded in December of 1979. They woke one morning to the sound of men shouting and an engine turning over, roaring to life. The soldiers were fleeing the camp. They'd received word from Angkar, and they were firing up the trucks and heading inland, trying to escape before the Vietnamese arrived.

All the boys ran along the road, unsure of what was happening and where they should go.

When the army actually arrived, they killed everyone in their path. Arun and my brother hid under the bodies they found alongside the road until the soldiers passed. Then they fled into the jungle at night, eating leaves to survive.

Entire villages were evacuating from the border. Sometimes they ran into groups of Khmer Rouge, but the soldiers were afraid to waste their bullets. The soldiers stole the lizard my brother was saving to eat later, the dead bat he'd found, the leaves Arun had picked. Finally they took the sandals off their feet, and then the soldiers went on. Sometimes Arun and my brother ran into families or just bands of lost children, wide-eyed and terrified, trying to find their way back to their parents' villages. If the children carried food, Arun and my brother asked for some. Once they simply took it from the children and ran.

Everyone was so hungry. It didn't seem like stealing. It didn't seem like a bad thing to do. It was food. But then, afterward, their stomachs hurt, they had cramping diarrhea. It seemed a funny time for Heaven to be showing any opinion about the business of man, but they didn't steal from children again after that.

Together they returned to the jungle, hiding during the day, and walking only at night, when it would be harder for people to see them. My brother no longer trusted people, no matter if they were soldiers or villagers; humans were dangerous, he decided. He'd take his chances with the animals and the minefields. They followed along the edges of a Khmer Rouge-built road, stepping on bodies when they saw them because they knew then that the mines would have already gone off. They hid in the brush, they hid under the bodies, they hid whenever they thought they heard people. Eventually they came upon a large group of men who were wearing civilian clothes but who still moved like soldiers, walking toward the Thai border. My brother didn't trust them, but he followed them at a distance, tracking them like animals. In this manner he was able to make it to a refugee camp in Thailand with Arun.

We're safe, my brother thought. We've made it.

But in the camp, he quickly learned they'd landed in a new kind of trouble. They were two boys without family, without protectors. The Red Cross doctors were able to save Arun from the infections that ravaged his body, but they could not heal the wounds he'd already suffered, the ones that no one could see. For several months Arun lost his sight, although the doctors said there was nothing wrong with his eyes. He felt mysterious pains and heard the voices of the dead in the wind. When his sight returned, the doctors accused him of having lied. Other survivors thought he was possessed by demons.

The camp directors tried to find a family that would take them in, but nobody wanted a sick boy. It was bad enough to have to take in a stranger's son, and they had enough burdens with their own children. If they took in a teenager, they wanted one who could work for them.

My brother sized up the families very quickly. Ones with many small children were the most vulnerable. He learned to ingratiate himself with the mothers, he learned to make himself useful. He protected them from the gangs of thieves that roved through the camp, from the crazies who had lost their minds in the war and now fought against phantoms with improvised weapons, from the bullies with small privileges doling out soup in the kitchens or helping the doctors in the makeshift hospitals. But still no family would take them in.

Then finally he figured out how to bargain with the fathers. *My father was a rich man*, he said. *He'll give you a big reward if you help me. My father was a member of Sihanouk's government, he had many foreign ties, he left the country before the Khmer Rouge took over and doesn't know what happened to me. When I find him again, he'll reward anyone who's helped me.*

To prove he wasn't lying, he told them stories about his life in the capital as a boy. He described the meals he ate, the servants he ordered about, the movies he'd seen, the toys he'd played with.

At last a family was willing to take them in.

After they were sponsored to come to America, my brother had to change his name, of course, so that all the papers matched. He and Arun became this family's paper sons, and my brother's real identity was lost. It was just another story he remembered, and no longer a person that Uncle could track through the Red Cross.

After he arrived in America, the family moved in with cousins in L.A., but they grew angry when my brother couldn't find his rich father. They made him work instead of going to school. Then he joined a gang to make some money, promised Arun he'd be back, but then he got caught and spent some time in juvenile detention, where he got his GED. When he got out again, he went to look for Arun. The family told him Arun had moved away.

My brother tried living on his own, here and there, trying to find work. But it wasn't easy. He had a record, he didn't have an education, he had gang tats. These were hard years. He started selling drugs again, then he saw the article in the paper. My brother glanced at the picture, then he stared. He almost couldn't believe it, just when he'd completely given up, there was his long-lost father, smiling in black and white from the front page.

His rich father, alive and well in America, in a town just down the 10.

It was a dream come true. Better than winning the lottery. It was like the happy ending of the sentimental movies Arun used to watch in Phnom Penh.

That very day, he packed up his belongings in his car and drove on the 10, leaving the city behind, and traveled all the way to Santa Bonita, a podunk little town he'd never heard of in the Inland Empire, to find the father he'd last seen when we was nine years old.

There was something missing from Paul's story. I couldn't put my finger on it, I couldn't say what exactly was wrong. But he was lying about something, hiding something important and big, so glaring I could feel it like a bruise pulsing just beneath my skin. But all I said was, "That's some story."

And Paul nodded, agreeing with me.

CHAPTER 15

On the Altar of Miracles

I had just managed to doze off when the phone rang, waking me from a half-dream in which I was driving on the highway, the taillights of the cars ahead of me streaming red light like water until I was floating down the 10 on a glowing crimson river. Giant fish—catfish, carp, a ribbony eel with a mouth full of teeth—and a white crocodile bobbed in the air beside me as I tried to steer around them. I found that I had an oar in my hands, and that I was paddling through a red-tinged fog. Someone honked at me, and I peered through the haze, desperately trying to see past the floating schools of fierce-looking fish, but the honking continued, and I woke up on the sofa, my neck cricked against its arm.

The phone rang again, and I leapt up, tripping over my feet as I ran to the kitchen. Maybe something had happened to Uncle, I thought, and I was suddenly chilled, my skin turning to gooseflesh in the gray light of early morning. "Hello?"

"Who is this?" A husky voice at the other end sounded angry.

"Are you calling for my uncle?" I asked.

"Your what?" There was a pause, and then the person hung up.

"Give me that!" Paul emerged from the bedroom and grabbed the receiver. "Hello? . . . Hello?" Disappointed, he slammed the receiver back on its cradle. "Who was that?"

"I don't know. The person hung up." I padded back to the sofa. "Don't wake up Sitan."

Sitan shifted on the floor, his sheets a knot around his legs. It was bad enough that Uncle allowed both Sitan and Paul to share his apartment, two men who were all but strangers to me, but now he didn't even bother to return, leaving us alone with each other. I curled up on the sofa, pulling my coat over my knees.

"Was it a woman? What exactly did she say?" Paul was wearing jeans, no socks, no shirt. His long torso was tattooed up and down. The light was too dim to see much of the design. A long eel or perhaps a dragon, something with scales and bulging eyes peered from between his washboard abs.

"It was a guy, I think," I whispered. "Maybe it was a woman. I don't know." I tried to find my comfortable spot again as I sank into the cushions.

"What did she say?" Paul was standing over me now. He grabbed hold of my shoulder and shook me.

"Hey! Hands off!" I shoved his hand away and jumped over the back of the sofa so the furniture was between us.

"Huh? What?" Sitan sat upright, his eyes still closed. He rubbed at his head with one hand.

"What did she say to you?" Paul spoke slowly, as though he thought I might be lying, as though there were a right and a wrong answer and he was threatening me to get it right.

"What the hell is wrong with you?" I gauged the distance around him to the door in case I had to run. He seemed unhinged, desperate. I climbed over the back of the couch, darted over to the kitchen phone, and dialed *27. The phone at the other end rang, and I held it out to Paul. "Ask her yourself."

Paul grabbed the phone. "Hello? . . . It's me! . . . Hello? Hello?"

"Call the operator. Trace the number, see who we just called."

Paul bounded into the bedroom and came back out, pulling on his T-shirt, then his leather jacket. He stuffed his bare feet into the sneakers by the door.

"Where you going?" I asked.

But he ran out without answering, slamming the door behind him.

By the time Uncle returned from supervising the baking, Sitan had taken off as well. Only I remained, seated in the kitchenette, eating half of the grapefruit.

Uncle smiled. "Put some sugar on," he urged me.

"I like it sour."

"Is he still sleeping?" He gestured toward the bedroom door. "I have a surprise when he wakes up. I spoke to Father Juan, and he is going to announce this miracle during Christmas Mass. I told him I would bring my family. All of us together. To thank God for this blessing. I almost lost faith that this day would ever come, but now I am so thankful." Uncle smiled.

I nodded, fairly certain that Paul would be less than thrilled with this surprise. "Paul went out a few hours ago."

"Where? Why?"

"I don't know. Someone, some woman I think, called and then hung up on him, and he got angry and left."

Uncle looked somber. He took off his jacket carefully and hung it on the back of his chair, his movements small and precise, as though too much motion might unsettle the balance of the universe.

"We can hit redial on the phone and see if he's there."

Uncle didn't answer. "He'll be back." He seemed to be trying to reassure himself. He put a paper bag on the table in front of me. "The Kasim sisters made *tarte aux fraises*."

"Thank you," I said. He nodded and headed to the bathroom.

I picked up the phone and hit redial, but the other end only rang and rang and rang. Whoever lived there didn't have an answering machine. Then I called the operator and asked if she could give me the last number I'd called. I thanked her and wrote it down on the side of the brown bag of pastry.

"Was it busy again this morning?" I called to Uncle through the bathroom door, but he didn't answer. I could hear the water running in the shower.

I really hoped Paul wasn't going to just disappear now that he'd turned up. Was he disappointed because Uncle wasn't rich anymore? Then a thought caused a chill to run up and down my spine. Maybe he really was just casing out the donut store. Maybe he hadn't left the gang. Now I wished I'd taken a better look at his tats. Maybe someone could identify what they meant, which gang he was affiliated with. The more I thought about it, the more naive I realized we'd been. We had no proof that this "Paul" was really my long-lost brother. Didn't he himself admit his records all had made-up names? The Red Cross wouldn't be able to say who he really was. And the story of his escape in Cambodia. How did I know it was true?

We didn't even have his DNA for a test, although I had no idea where anyone actually tested DNA except for crime labs on TV cop shows.

I looked in the sink, but there wasn't so much as an unwashed cup.

Nothing to prove Paul was who he said he was.

And nothing to find him with again if he didn't come back.

At work, I hinted to Anita that Paul was an imposter. "Did you ever see a picture of my family? There was one taken in Phnom Penh," I said. "I saw it once, when Uncle lived with us in Nebraska."

"I don't think I have, honey. But I sure would like to if you find it."

"So you don't actually know what Paul is supposed to look like? Because he doesn't look like Uncle, does he? He's strong-looking. He's got broad shoulders and all those muscles. He's not very tall. Uncle used to look, not exactly handsome, but like a wealthy man. He had that kind of never-had-to-work-in-his-life look."

"That must have been some photograph," Anita said.

"What if there's some kind of mistake?"

"Your uncle is so happy, honey," Anita said. "Finding his son alive is the answer to his prayers."

"But what if Paul isn't really who he says he is? What if he's lying?"

"Now why would I think a thing like that?" Anita shook her head. "Sometimes we just have to have faith."

The next day came and went. Uncle stayed open on Christmas Eve, just in case Paul should try to find him there at the donut shop.

"I'm sure he's busy," Uncle said. "Something came up. He has his own life. I should have told him my plans. I forgot that he is a grown man. He has this girlfriend who called him. Maybe he has his own family. I didn't ask. I didn't think to ask. Maybe he thinks I don't care. Maybe he's disappointed in me. I didn't think."

"I'm sure he'll come back," I said, Uncle's state of agitation alarming me. I'd never seen him this nervous. Ma's mood swings I was used to, but I hadn't known Uncle to question his blind faith in the future before, and it worried me.

"You think he'll come back?" Uncle asked, as though he genuinely cared about my answer.

"Yes," I said.

"He said he's coming back?"

"Well, I didn't ask. He didn't say good-bye. It seemed like he was just going out for a bit."

"Maybe he's been injured. Maybe something has happened."

"He'll come back. He found you. He gave your number to his friends to call, didn't he? That means he wanted them to know he was here." I didn't add, So that after he cased the place, he could signal for them to rob us. But then I felt guilty for even thinking it. Again.

"I'll pray. The Lord has been so good to me. I won't be ungrateful."

On Christmas, Uncle insisted I go with him to church.

"But won't Father be expecting Paul? He'll be disappointed if it's only me."

"No, the miracle is the same even if Ponleu is not here today," Uncle insisted. "I am still thankful. I am still grateful. And if we don't come, then Father will be disappointed."

I hadn't brought any fancy clothes. So for Christmas morning, rather than my usual jeans, I put on the one pair of khakis I'd packed in my backpack. They were a cotton-poly blend and not too wrinkled. And I had a snap-up Western-style blouse with red embroidered roses on it that the twins had given me for my birthday. I tried to put more attention into my eye makeup, as though that might help, but after my best efforts, the woman peering back at me from the bathroom mirror still looked kind of like a rodeo queen on a bad day. I sighed. It was the best I could do on short notice and no money.

Uncle emerged from his bedroom in a baggy gray suit, not the nicer one from the newspaper photo. He'd lost weight since Auntie's death. I imagined him wearing the same suit at her memorial service, and tried not to shudder.

"You look good," Uncle said, smiling.

I thought about all the ways I could refute that, but instead I simply said, "Thank you."

Then we left for church.

The last time I'd been in a church, my older sister Sourdi was a teen bride in an arranged marriage. Just thinking about it made me angry again. As Uncle drove, I tried to concentrate on my breathing, in through the nostrils, out through the mouth, like the counselors in school said to do. I focused on the present, not the could-have-beens. Sourdi was happy. She loved her three children. It was her life, her choices, not my decisions to make.

Uncle pulled in to the gravel lot behind the small white church, nodding as though he'd decided something, come to a kind of agreement with his conscience or God or whatever voice in his head that he talked to and expected answers from. Meanwhile, my heart beat faster, my palms went clammy. My attempts at positive thinking weren't working. I had bad church memories.

After we were sponsored by the First Baptists in a small town in Texas, the Church Ladies would come to the trailer park to pick us up and take us to church. People nudged each other in the pews, recognizing the clothes on our backs as we walked down the aisle. Everything we had in those days had been donated from the congregation. Later, Ma would refuse to go, claiming headaches or mysterious illnesses; she couldn't bear the stares, the way they made her feel guilty. Sponsoring our family had been the minister's idea. Not everybody in the church felt America needed another refugee family, but now the congregation was responsible for us—for renting the trailer we lived in, for finding Ma the maid's job at the Motel 6. Without out their sponsorship, the government wouldn't have granted us visas. Ma said we should be grateful to them, but that didn't make everyone in the church any happier. We were clearly a burden.

I didn't know any English at first, didn't know what people were whispering, but I could understand the suspicion in their sidelong glances, the ridicule in the way kids tugged at the corners of their eyes, the condescension from the Minister's Wife when she clapped her hand on our shoulders tight as a vise. Like we belonged to her, like we were her pets or exotic animals to display.

As I followed Uncle through the heavy wooden doors, the smell of incense and sweat mixed in the air. The somber organ music was heavy like a hand on the back of my neck. I felt my chest tighten and my throat constrict. I recognized the signs that I might be going into a panic attack. Breathe, breathe, breathe, I thought.

Uncle was still muttering to himself as he walked up the middle aisle, seemingly oblivious to the gaze of the congregants. They evidently had all heard the good news. Row after row of families decked out in their Christmas best turned toward Uncle, toothy smiles lighting up their faces. They could have been sunflowers at dawn, the way their heads rose and turned as he approached. Out of the corners of my eyes, I could see their puzzled looks as we passed, the nudges. They were waiting for the son. They were wondering who I was. And suddenly the panicked thought came to me that maybe they thought I was the son. I was thin, my hair short still. Did I look like a really effeminate guy? I wondered. Were they staring at me?

I hadn't felt this uncomfortable since my first day of school in Texas, when all the kids stared at me and Sourdi. A girl in ESL turned in her seat to make a face at Sourdi. The fights on the schoolyard. That feeling that I was walking with a target on my forehead. Now I forced myself to look straight ahead and ignore the people, staring only at the altar bedecked in red poinsettias. Their foil-covered pots scattered the candlelight like so many tears falling at our feet.

I reminded myself that I need not feel afraid anymore. In this church, the congregants were Uncle's friends, or at least people who knew him, people he'd helped. If they were staring, it was because they were excited for him, his good news printed in the bulletin for everyone to see: "James Chhouen has been blessed by God. His eldest son, missing since the take-over of the Khmer Rouge in Cambodia, is alive and well and is reunited with him. Join us in prayers of thanks at the 11 a.m. Mass, Christmas Day."

Uncle took a seat at the very front of the church in the first pew. If Father Juan was surprised to see only me seated next to Uncle, he did not let it show on his face. He smiled and nodded at Uncle as he said the Mass. We rose and sat and knelt and rose again, the ritual of the movements soothing my nerves.

Then, during the homily, I saw Father Juan look right at us and smile, and my heart tightened. I thought he would make us stand up in the glare of everyone's eyes, but he only talked about "God's miraculous love," and spoke in the most abstract terms about Uncle finding his son. Perhaps Uncle had not told him the details, or perhaps they were not important. It only mattered that Uncle's faith in God had been restored.

When I was ten, just before Ma decided to leave our small town for a better job in East Dallas, she insisted that all of us children become born-again. She wanted to pay back our sponsors. In exchange for their kindness, she was giving them our souls. We were baptized before the entire congregation. I remembered standing on the side of the altar, dripping wet in a borrowed white robe and blinking the water out of my eyes, as all those smiling faces came up to congratulate the Pastor and his wife. Teeth snapped at the air, sharklike, circling round us children. This is what bait feels like, I thought. This is what it's like to be a worm on a hook, waiting to see which fish will bite first.

Now I held my body rigid with expectation, with the fear of being observed and judged for some deficit that I'd been previously unaware I possessed. This was what it felt like to be a refugee. To be on display, uncertain of myself, in a room full of staring people. I clenched my jaw so tightly that even my teeth hurt. I had hoped that I'd outgrow this feeling someday, that college would somehow change me, transform me into the confident American who always felt she belonged, but here I was, reliving my ten-year-old self all over again.

I was lost in my memories, not paying attention to Uncle, when I heard a strange gasping sound. I turned and discovered he was crying, his eyes squeezed shut, tears pouring down his face, falling over his sharp cheekbones. I didn't have any pockets, I couldn't offer him any tissues, but another parishioner was fast on the draw, digging in her purse for a pack of Kleenex and then surreptitiously pushing it into his hand. I watched Uncle wipe the tears away.

After Mass, people came up to Uncle, smiles on their faces, congratulating him. "I'm so happy you found your son!" "What a blessing!" "Alleluia! God has answered your prayers!" They patted his back, grabbed his sleeve, grasped his arm.

Uncle nodded, smiling.

Before anyone could approach and attempt to strike up a conversation, I stepped back from the crowd and pretended I was fascinated by the rows of votive candles. I didn't want to have to explain who I was, and I didn't want to lie to strangers.

And, for a moment, I could actually believe that everything would turn out perfectly well, that this happiness could last, and that there might somehow be enough left over to encompass me.

Kneeling before the flickering flames, the smoke and incense filling my nostrils, I had the curious sensation that I was floating, observing everyone from the high vaulted ceiling. I looked down on the heads of the people below me as they flowed toward Uncle like a river, splitting and dividing around him as though he were a rock in their path. The light from the stained-glass windows spilled around me in bands of blue and green and yellow. I dipped my open palm into a stream of red light from the sunlight pouring through the image depicting Christ carrying a cross on his shoulder, his face twisted in agony. The red glass panels around his head might have been blood or flame, I couldn't be sure, but I held the light in my hand, then squeezed my fingers into a fist, as though I could capture the light and save it for later use. I floated overhead, watching the people patting Uncle on the back, shaking his hand. An old woman with blue-white cataracts clouding her eyes marched up to him and grabbed hold of his jacket, rubbing it between her thumb and forefinger as though she were a character in a parable, expecting to be healed by the power invested in the hem of a prophet's garment.

That night, I decided to call Ma from the pay phone near the bus stop. Uncle had been talking on the phone nearly nonstop since we'd come home from church. Everyone was calling him to offer congratulations, to wish him a Merry Christmas, to share their own stories. He talked on and on, apparently having the same conversation over and over. Finally I decided not to wait for the calls to end, stuffed my wallet in the pocket of my hoodie, and slipped outside.

The night air was chilly, and I wrapped my arms around my chest as I ran down the sidewalk. There was very little traffic out—everyone was at home with their families—and the night seemed darker and somehow colder for the lack of cars and people. I could see the blinking lights wrapped around the front of the apartment building, and a few Christmas trees lit up the dark windows. A bench by the phone booth advertised the latest holiday blockbuster, but the stars' teeth had long been blackened by vandals, the smiling Santa tagged. The giant "Ho, Ho, Ho!" no longer seemed festive now that it was surrounded by obscenities and a giant arrow that suggested it was a slur against any woman who should happen to sit on the bench.

I pulled out my quarters and laid them carefully atop the metal phone. As I dropped them into the slot, I practiced what I would say in case Ma wanted to know how preparations for the internship interview were going ("Busy!") or what I'd done that day (church and then dinner with my roommate's family) and a wild card—what if she asked to speak to my roommate's mother? Ma was pretty confident in her English nowadays. She might just want to check to see if I was behaving myself. I decided I'd tell her that the parents were opening presents and that's why I'd stepped away to call her.

I waited while the phone rang and rang. Then Marie's cheerful voice answered: "Hello?"

"Marie! Merry Chris—"

"You've reached the Chhim residence. Sorry we had to miss your call, but please leave a message! We'll get right back to you!"

There was a long beep.

"Hi, Ma! Marie, Jennifer, Sam! Merry Christmas! It's Nea!" I realized that sounded stupid. I tried again, "I miss you all! I hope you had a great day. It's really cool out here in California. I mean, it's actually kind of warm, but that's what's cool. There's a big palm tree right in front of me and—" The phone beeped a second time and cut me off.

I decided to call the Palace and fished out more quarters. Ma used to keep the restaurant open every holiday when I was growing up. She'd backed off after the twins started high school, allowing them to take one major holiday off, but maybe she'd changed her mind this year. I pressed the phone to my ear, hoping, as I listened to the familiar ring.

Then it was Sam's deep voice: "You've reached the Silver Palace. Leave a message after the beep."

"Merry Christmas, everybody!" I called into the answering machine, just in case they were screening the calls. But nobody came to answer. I left my greetings, then hung up.

Walking back to the apartment, I practiced my smile in the dark. I didn't want Uncle to see how I felt. I didn't want my loneliness to ruin his happy day.

PART SIX

If you see a tiger crouching, don't assume it's kowtowing to you.

—traditional Cambodian proverb

CHAPTER 16

The Day After

When I was eleven and we were all living together in Nebraska, trying to make the Silver Palace a success, Uncle used to like to talk about the miracles he'd witnessed in Phnom Penh when he was growing up. The canary that learned to sing in Khmer. The new year fireworks that had lasted for three weeks, exploding continuously without ever having to be re-lit. The windstorm that had sent the nuns who taught at his lycée tumbling into the sky on the very day he'd prayed for a miracle because he hadn't had time to prepare for an important exam. He'd arrived at the school to discover the nuns flying through the air, blown away by the storm, and classes cancelled while the laymen raced on bicycles, chasing the nuns to see where they would land.

Perhaps Uncle was used to miracles, but they made me nervous as a kid. I kept waiting for the day after, when we had to keep living the rest of our lives.

The day after Christmas, business was better than ever at the donut shop. Uncle called me and asked if I could take the bus in to work. He apologized, said he couldn't step away even to pick me up. There were that many customers.

"It's a true miracle from God," Uncle said. I could hear voices in the background, it sounded like singing. I could barely hear what Uncle said next, but it sounded like, "Is your brother back?"

But then there was a loud voice and he was distracted, telling someone the price of the palmières, and even though I said,
"What did you say? I couldn't hear you," over and over, loudly,
into the receiver, he hung up without saying anything more.

Had he slipped and referred to Paul as my brother? Or was
I merely imagining what I'd wanted him to say?

I threw on a sweatshirt and jeans and ran a comb through
my hair. I jumped into my shoes, grabbed my backpack by the
door, and ran all the way to the bus stop. I was so excited. So
eager.

Even before the bus stopped, I could see the line wending its
way around the donut shop, through the parking lot, and down
the sidewalk of the strip mall, past the grocery, the Copy Circle,
the video store, and the tanning salon. I hadn't realized until
this moment how a priest's word of a miracle would be good
for business, how one man's found son might inspire hope for
other wishes to come true: a marriage repaired, a lottery won,
a wound healed. I had forgotten how people in a small, poor
community would bank on the hope that luck was contagious.

I ran in the back entrance through the kitchen, where the
fans were whirring nonstop and the Kasim sisters were still
working, showing a group of teenage girls how to knead dough.
I greeted them with a *sompeah* and a smile, hung my coat on a
hook on the wall, then ran into the front room where customers were lined up patiently as Uncle dispensed the remaining
donuts and pastries, one each, into white paper bags and Anita
rang up the purchases. Uncle was explaining to one woman
how he'd prayed every day for ten years, longer, and finally his
prayers were answered. "If only my wife had lived to see this
day," he said, "but I know she sees from Heaven and she is smiling." The woman clutched the bag with the donut in it to her
chest and nodded, tears welling up in her eyes. She grabbed
hold of his hand and whispered something I couldn't quite

make out. "I'm sure your prayers will be answered, too," Uncle told her. "Look at me. I am proof."

I sidled up to Anita at the cash register. "Glad you're here, Nea. Your uncle's been working nonstop. If he doesn't take a break, I'm afraid he's going to drop!"

"I can't believe all these people are here. We could charge double," I whispered.

"Oh, hush. It's all I can do to keep your uncle from giving the donuts away." But then Anita winked, so I figured she must have managed to talk him out of that plan. Plus, it was a good sign that someone had called the Kasim sisters and the bakers. Thinking ahead, trying to keep the pastry in stock, training new workers. Business was going so well, I almost couldn't believe it.

If only Paul were there, I knew Uncle would be perfectly happy.

Where that left me, I wasn't sure.

By sunset, around five, it was just Sitan and me manning the counter. Anita had finally convinced Uncle that he needed to rest. All the Nicorette, Sudafed, and caffeine in the world could only go so far. The crowd, however, had not thinned. In fact, it seemed that coming for miracle donuts was supplanting the return of gifts as *the* Day After Christmas activity of choice. Sitan and I had taken to selling the donut holes one at a time to make them last, but when I saw that we'd clearly be out of pastry, I ran up and down the line outdoors telling people they'd have to come back tomorrow. I handed out a flyer that I'd quickly made up at the copy shop: "Come back tomorrow! Fresh pastry! Hear about the miracle LIVE!" I'd included our operating hours and phone number and a coupon for catering, which I wasn't sure if Uncle ever wanted to offer, but it seemed like a good idea, like something to branch into.

Now as I stood next to Sitan as he bagged up the last three donut holes, I could see the rest of the people outside staring inside. Our shop was the brightest thing in the strip mall, our fluorescent lights bouncing off the linoleum and the white walls. I felt like a fish in an aquarium, exposed to eyes that I couldn't even see. The sun had long set, and darkness had settled suddenly on the parking lot, the few streetlights sparking to life, their bulbs glowing dimly like small yellow candles on a large dark cake. They cast a crooked triangle of light throughout the parking lot, but not directly onto the sidewalk in front of the donut shop. People emerged from the darkness into the bright white lights of our windows and peered wide-eyed at us inside. I felt bad when I had to tell them we were finally out of donuts, but at least nobody got angry. They clutched the flyers I handed them, nodded without arguing, and marched away into the dark parking lot, some of them heading toward the bus stop across the street. I guess people who were looking for a miracle had a particular kind of patience.

I was wiping down the counters while Sitan filled up the mop bucket in the back when there was a sharp rap on the glass door. A baby-faced little boy smiled back at me.

I pointed to the "Closed" sign, and he pointed to his mouth and shook his head.

I wiped my hands on my jeans and went to open the door. "I'm sorry, we're all sold out today. You'll have to come tomorrow when we're open."

The kid shook his head at me. Suddenly two men in ski masks ran up to the door, shoved me hard so that I fell backward into the shop, and slammed the door behind me.

One of them grabbed me by the arm and threw me against the counter. "Open the cash register, bitch," and I felt a sharp metal something jammed up hard against my ribs.

I tried not to panic. Everything seemed too bright. I could see the empty counters, the dishrag on the Formica, the black metal of the register.

"Hurry up, bitch, or you're dead." The man's voice was slurred, breathy.

My ears were ringing, hypersensitive. I could hear the water in the pipes, the traffic on the street, the hum of the fluorescent lights. Only my heart was gone. I couldn't hear its beat.

I wanted to warn Sitan, who had gone into the kitchen, but I couldn't speak. I pressed "sale," but the register wouldn't open. I tried again.

"Hurry up!" the man growled.

Sitan emerged from the back carrying the bucket and the long-handled mop. The second man lifted a piece of pipe he'd been carrying and ran at Sitan.

"No, wait! Here's the money! Here!" I shouted, finding my voice at last. The cash door sprang open, and I waved a fistful of cash in the air.

The second man hit Sitan, who fell to the floor. I screamed and, remembering Anita's knives, I patted around on the shelf under the counter till I felt the edges of the wooden box. I snapped the lid open and pulled out a long blade. The metal was cold under my fingers, surprisingly heavy, but the weight well balanced. It felt lethal. "Get out!" I shouted, and threw the knife. It whizzed through the air, missing both men by a good three feet and striking the Christmas tree with a *thwack*, but at least I got the second man's attention. He stopped hitting Sitan. I grabbed another knife, and even Sitan ducked this time.

"Crazy bitch!" The thug crouched, holding up his arms like a shield before his face. "Let's go!"

The first man grabbed the cash from the register. He pointed the metal pipe directly at my head. "Watch it, tiger girl."

I raised another knife, held it between us, and then, narrowing my eyes, aimed at his head. "Grr," I said, threatening to throw it.

The two men ran out the front door.

Blood gushed down Sitan's face. He clutched his head with both hands.

I pulled some napkins from the dispenser and handed them to Sitan. I ran to the front door and locked it. I ran to the back door and locked it.

Someone was screaming. I assumed it was Sitan, but when I ran back into the front room, Sitan was standing quietly, patting his head with the napkins.

I swallowed, and the screaming stopped.

"I'm calling an ambulance! Don't move!" I said.

"S'alright. Don't call an ambulance. It's just a cut."

"You're bleeding all over the place!"

"I can't afford an ambulance." Sitan kicked the wall, then kicked the kitchen door. It swung into the bucket and dumped it over, spilling soapy water all over the linoleum. "I can't believe it. I let myself be sucker punched like that."

I called 911. "I'm calling to report a robbery. At Happy Donuts. Six-two-five-five El Camino Boulevard. There were two armed men. And a kid. I think the kid was part of it—"

"Slow down, miss." The dispatcher's voice was unimpressed. "What exactly happened now?"

"Armed robbery. Two men. My friend's hurt. He's bleeding. A lot. There's blood everywhere."

She seemed happier to hear that. Or at least more alert. "I'll send an ambulance."

"Don't send an ambulance. Just the cops. I mean, the police."

"If he's hurt, I've got to send an ambulance."

"He's gonna drive himself to the hospital. Actually, he's already going. Just send the police."

Then the operator wanted to know what the men had looked like, and I realized I couldn't tell her. "They had ski masks."

"You got any closed-circuit security cameras?"

"No. I don't think so." I looked around the donut shop, hoping there were security cameras I'd never noticed before, but no. No cameras. Nothing.

"Just stay there. Don't let your friend go. I'm sending a squad car."

I was shaking by the time the cops arrived. Furious at myself. I must have lost my edge in college. I'd forgotten to always keep an eye open, to never let my guard down. Now I couldn't identify the robbers; I didn't remember what they were wearing beyond the black ski masks and the heavy dark puffer jackets, the jeans. I wasn't sure of how tall they were, their weight, their ethnicity. I couldn't even tell the police how much money they'd stolen. We hadn't had time yet to count the day's take.

"Most important thing is you're okay," the first police officer said after I'd given my worthless account. "Staying alive, staying healthy, that's the important thing. I always say, Don't play a hero. That's how you end up dead."

"Well, I didn't play any hero." To my surprise, I suddenly burst into tears. Hot angry tears, the kind I used to cry when I had a fight with Ma, when she wouldn't listen to me, when she acted as though all my efforts to help were a burden.

"It's okay, miss," the second officer said. "This is the kind of ending we like. Where everybody's alive. This is the happy ending, as far as we're concerned."

I nodded and tried to smile, but this wasn't the happy ending I'd been imagining. This wasn't happy at all, and I turned my face to the wall so they wouldn't see me crying, wouldn't see how my face turned red and splotchy, how my eyes swelled up, how my nose ran like a snot faucet.

I couldn't help but feel I'd screwed the whole day up.

"There was a kid," I said, remembering just as the police were going to leave. "He was this high." I held my hand just below my shoulder. I didn't know if he was white or just pale.

The police gave me the report number so I could call if I remembered any more important details, and I knew then that this was the end of it.

There was nothing to do after the police left but to finish cleaning up. Sitan didn't want to go to the hospital; he said he was fine, and there was no convincing him otherwise. So I said I'd tell Uncle the bad news when I went back to the apartment. Sitan put the boom box on full volume and turned the dial to a rap station so we could clean to the angry growl of N.W.A.

"You know, it's kinda funny. I used to belong to a gang," Sitan said, pushing the mop in rhythm to "Straight Out of Compton."

"You mentioned that." Sitan with his round Buddha face and his gentle smile. I couldn't imagine him carrying a gun or a knife, threatening to hurt people, but I also didn't know him very well.

"Sold crack for a while, too," he said. "That was a messed-up time for me."

"Is that when you met your girlfriend?"

"Naw. Afterwards. That's why her parents didn't trust me. They thought I was some gangbanger. They know my brother's in prison. They figured I'd end up there, too."

"They'll come around," I said. "They'll see you've changed."

"I wanted a family, you know? I thought the gang was where it was at. I thought: These are my brothers. They'll look out for me. I'll look out for them. That's what they want you to think," he said. "But they really just thought I was some stupid little kid who'd do anything they said. Didn't see that until too late. I got arrested. I got a record now. And now my girlfriend's parents think I'm no good." He methodically dipped the mop in the bucket, wrung it out on the side, dipped it in again, wrung the liquid out of the filthy yarn head. "I had to leave Lillian with her mother again today. I know what her parents are thinking. They think I can't support my own kid." He mopped the floor now as though he were plowing a field

Sitan reminded me of my brother, Sam. They both struck me as fundamentally lonely. I thought of Sam working prep, sitting alone in the kitchen of the Palace slicing carrots, dicing bell peppers, all his athleticism concentrated in the smooth, precise chops of his knife. He'd grown used to being the only Cambodian boy in our town. He'd dropped out of wrestling; he hadn't been able to find any new friends in that too-small town. No wonder he wanted to join the army, I thought. All those promises of finding an entire band of brothers. I wished he could meet Sitan, but then I'd have to admit to Ma that I'd lied, that I'd come here to find Uncle. I didn't see how I could arrange one without the other, and I wasn't ready to face Ma's anger.

"You're a really good father, Sitan," I said.

Sitan put the mop down on the floor and straightened up. He looked me straight in the eye, his face very serious. "You really think that?"

"Yes. I've seen how you talk to your daughter even though she's so small, just like she can understand."

"I know she can understand!"

"And you're always thinking about her. Always talking about her. You're a very considerate father."

Sitan seemed to think about that. "Con-si-der-ate. I like that." He nodded, and the peaceful Buddha smile returned. "Thank you, Nea. I'm going to tattoo that on my arm someday. That's exactly who I want to be."

Before I knew what was happening, he leaned over quickly and kissed me on the cheek, and then, now that he had my attention, on the mouth. I had just enough time to taste his lips, the salt of his blood, and feel the soft pulse beneath his flesh, when he pulled away, embarrassed.

Then he picked up the boom box and wheeled the bucket into the kitchen. I finished wiping up the counters and the soda machines and the pastry and donut trays, the beat of his angry music pulsing through the wall like a rapidly beating heart.

That night Uncle took the robbery in stride. "The important thing is you're safe. And Sitan is safe. God be praised. Another miracle." Then he said a prayer of thanks in the apartment, facing the cross he'd nailed to the wall that afternoon under the framed picture of Angkor Wat. I wondered how Uncle reconciled his vision of a benevolent deity who kept people safe from robbers in a donut shop but didn't protect people from a murderous regime in an entire country. It didn't seem fair or just or commonsensical to me, but it wasn't my faith, it was his, and it seemed to give him the incredible energy he needed for the donut shop and his volunteer work and church and praying. I still couldn't understand how he could sleep so little and do so much.

I felt lazy in comparison. No, that was too mild. I felt, in truth, utterly exhausted.

I sat on the couch in the living room, my back aching, my legs limp, my feet swollen from having stood all day and into the night, but Uncle was pacing excitedly in the apartment, from the window by the kitchen past the couch to the front door and back, praying with his hands in the air. I knew I should try to make something for dinner. There were eggs in the fridge and some leftover takeout and frozen waffles in the freezer, if I remembered correctly. Next thing I knew I'd passed out completely. I only realized I'd fallen asleep the moment I woke up.

Blinking, I tried to remember where I was. In my dream, I had been working in the Palace, which had morphed into a Chinese restaurant that sold donuts decorated with crucifixes made out of red spun sugar. The dining room was huge, all the tables packed with hungry customers, families with crying babies and children who wouldn't sit down but instead ran around the tables dropping small battery-powered toys with wheels, trying to trip me as I carried a full tray above my head. The fire alarm went off and I was suddenly in the kitchen, wielding a tiny red fire extinguisher. Every time I squeezed the nozzle, no foam came out, and the alarm bell rang on and on and on.

Then I realized it was the phone ringing.

The shower was running. It was dark in the apartment, an arc of yellow light spilling from Uncle's room. Uncle was getting ready to go to work again. It must've been time for him to supervise the bakers.

I struggled to my feet, rubbing my eyes. I stumbled toward the phone on the bookshelf against the wall and managed to stub my toe against the bottom shelf.

Yelping, I picked up the phone. "Yow, hello?"

"Is my father there?"

It was Paul.

"Where have you been? We were all worried—"

"I need to speak to my father."

"Hold your horses. He's in the shower. Where are you?"

There was a pause. "I'm with a friend."

"You know, Uncle was really disappointed. He had the priest say a special Mass for you—"

"Why? What's the matter?" Paul seemed genuinely alarmed.

"He wanted to thank God for the miracle of your safe return." Prodigal asshole, I thought, but I did not say it.

"Oh. That." Paul's voice was relieved. "Can you bang on his door or something? I'm in a hurry."

You have some nerve, I thought. "I can take a message."

"You tell him I want to speak to him. Now."

"You should call during normal business hours—"

Suddenly Uncle was at my elbow. I felt a damp hand on my shoulder and he took the phone from me.

"Ponleu, is it you?" he asked. A silence, then he was nodding and making soft, assenting sounds. "Mmm, mm-hmm. Mmm." Paul must have been doing most of the talking.

After he hung up, Uncle was overjoyed. "Your brother's coming back tomorrow. He called to let me know. He was concerned that I would be worried. It's very thoughtful of him."

Thoughtful? I thought. Why didn't he call these two days if he's so thoughtful? But all I said was, "Did he say where he went?"

"He apologized for leaving so quickly. He said he is coming back to help me run the business."

I could have pointed out that Paul was essentially asking for a job but acting like he was doing Uncle a favor. I didn't know where he got his arrogance from. Was this what a rich boy grew up to be like? Or was this the way a grifter behaved, reeling in his prey?

"You should rest now. You worked so hard. And the robbery. The police. Try to rest." Uncle was putting on his jacket, getting ready to return to the donut shop. There was a spring to his step. He adjusted the collar of his coat, patted the hair covering his bald spot. He snapped his Nicorette.

"I'm sorry I let the thieves get all our money," I said forlornly.

"God is good. He is watching out for us." Uncle smiled and waved as he went out the front door. "He brought your brother home, after all."

I sat in the dark on the sofa, too tired to get up and turn on a light or the TV or the radio. My body still ached. Sitting alone, listening to the sound of the traffic on the street outside, I felt sorry for myself. I was wishing that Uncle had acted as happy to see me as he had been to find this man who claimed to be his son when I realized Uncle had called Paul "your brother."

My heart beat faster. Was Uncle just speaking casually, using kinship terms loosely, the way all cousins can be called brothers and sisters, all adults can be a younger person's aunt or uncle? Or did he slip up and reveal how he really saw me, how he thought of me? And was this happiness of his not just reserved for the return of his missing son, but for the coalescing of his broken family, of both me and Paul?

It was hard to say with Uncle.

He was like Ma in this way. She never told me what she was really thinking. She endured, she worked, she grew angry and silent, she grew happy and whistled, but she never shared with me the inner workings of her heart. I was left to observe her moods and try to fit them together like pieces of a puzzle whose final design I could only guess at.

Thinking of my mother, I felt guilty for lying to her, telling her I was visiting my roommate's family, looking for a summer internship. I should have called her again, but I was afraid she'd hear the lies in my voice. She'd see through me and I'd confess everything. What if she insisted I come home immediately? I wasn't ready.

I felt alone and afraid, with no one to tell my fears and thoughts to. Because of the lie, I'd never be able to tell her about the robbery, never tell her how afraid I felt. I'd have to keep this lie between us our whole lives. I hadn't thought of that when I decided to come out here for winter break.

I missed Sam and the twins. Would I ever tell them if I didn't tell Ma? I shook my head. It would be wrong to burden them with my secrets. Sam was graduating high school this year; this was his last Christmas home, and I'd missed it. The twins were growing up, too. They had taken up cheerleading in an attempt to develop a talent for the pageant circuit. Ma had told me about it in our last conversation before I left: "They are driving me crazy, all this jumping and shouting." I didn't remind Ma that she'd never allowed Sourdi or me to participate in any sports or after-school activities. She kept us working in the Palace all the time, yet still she had complained about us and the trouble she felt we caused her. "Your sisters, it's all one-two-three-four who you gonna tell she ate." I didn't tell Ma she was missing a few words there, that the rhyme wasn't about eating at all. Ma had sighed on the phone. "Now you're all grown up. You can find your own work. You don't worry about your mother." She hadn't said, I miss you, I want you to come home and help me. I knew she did, but it wasn't the kind of thing she'd ever say out loud.

I pulled my knees to my chest and let myself cry. It felt good to sit in the dark on the lumpy sofa and wallow in self-pity. It'd been a long day, a scary day. I cried a little harder, let my tears slide down my cheeks and pool on the edges of my lips. They were warm and salty on the tip of my tongue. I tried sobbing out loud, letting little barking cries emerge from the back of my throat. I sounded a little like a circus seal, and decided to stop. Then my nose started to run, and I had to get up from the sofa and find some Kleenex to blow my nose. I rummaged in the bathroom, my eyes squinting from the bright light, and caught a glimpse of myself in the mirror over the sink. My makeup was running, my eyes were red, my nose looked swollen, snot glistened on my chin. Crying in the dark, I'd imagined myself like a heroine in a novel, like an actress in a TV show, artful tears catching the light, my quivering lips the portrait of inner pain, but in fact I looked like hell. I looked like a crazy person.

Quickly, I washed my face. I blew my nose. I stopped crying.

No point making things worse, I thought, and I went to bed.

CHAPTER 17

Sacred Heart

Paul reappeared in the early afternoon. I almost didn't notice him. We were having another boffo day, with even more customers than the day before. We had the customers who'd read about us in the paper and the people who'd heard from Father Juan about the Miracle and random passersby who'd noticed the lines from the street and pulled into the strip mall to see what was up. I told Anita we should put a limit on how much any one customer could buy—that way we could cut out any wannabe scalpers and keep customers enticed.

I was waiting for Sitan to come in the afternoon to take over for Anita when I saw Paul through the front window. He was watching the line of customers, maybe counting them for all I knew, his eyes narrowed as though calculating profits. He looked quite handsome, I realized, now that he wasn't trying to dress like a gang member, and instead had put on a fitted jacket over a button-up shirt and dark gray khaki slacks. Wherever he'd gone, he'd picked up some better clothes and cleaned up at least. I saw several of the women in the line glance at him curiously, wondering who he was. With his high cheekbones, straight nose, narrow eyes, and thick black hair brushed neatly to the side, he could have been a Hong Kong movie star slumming incognito in Southern California. He had that kind of air. I found him arrogant, but I could see how others might think him merely confident or even charismatic, someone who was used to being looked at.

Then the crowd shifted, and I saw a beautiful Khmer woman standing next to him. She *really* looked like a movie star. She had long, highlighted hair, which she flipped over her shoulder periodically. She was wearing a lot of makeup— bright red lipstick, thick black false eyelashes—and round sunglasses. When she spoke, Paul turned to her with a face like a little boy's—open and attentive and full of love.

I stared, mouth agape, until Anita poked me in the arm. "Earth to Nea, how ya doing there? Ready to ring up this woman's order?"

I blinked and turned; I tried to focus on the customers inside the shop, but they looked so ordinary. Nurses in scrubs, mothers with strollers, some men from the construction team down the street. Everyone looked tired and grumpy and frazzled. After seeing Paul and his girlfriend, I felt as though I'd been blinded by looking at the sun.

They were that glamorous.

I tried to ring up the order at the cash register, but ended up making a mistake and had to void the purchase. When I was finally finished, I looked out the window again but couldn't see Paul or his girlfriend. They'd simply disappeared.

"Did you see them? Paul was right there. With some woman," I told Anita.

"Tell him to come in. We could use an extra pair of hands or two," she said. "I can handle things for a few minutes while you go get them."

I ran outside, but they weren't in line, neither in the part in front of the donut shop nor in the part snaking down the strip mall. I ran into the parking lot, but I didn't see Paul's Mazda either. I didn't see how I could have imagined them;

there was no one in line that looked remotely like the couple I'd seen.

I figured they'd have to come back later. There was no reason to just stand outside the donut shop and not come in. Maybe they were waiting for Uncle to return, I thought.

Then, as I ran back inside, my terrible thoughts returned. What a coincidence that on our biggest day of sales ever, we should be robbed. And then today, Paul comes to check out business again. What if he were still tied up with criminals in some way, obligated to find new marks for them?

I shivered. I didn't want to be robbed again. Especially by family.

Anita was bagging up another half-dozen donut holes when I sidled up. "We should get security cameras. We should at least put up a sign saying we have hidden security cameras."

"It's natural to be nervous after what you and Sitan went through."

"I mean it, Anita. We should be prepared. I don't trust him."

"Sitan?" Anita looked surprised.

"No! Paul."

"Oh, honey. You don't know him yet."

"He was there, now he's gone. What's he watching us for? We don't really know anything about him. He shows up, we get robbed. He shows up again. I'm just sayin'."

Anita took a damp rag and wiped it across the counter top while the next group of customers stared at the cases, trying to decide what to order. "All I know is your uncle had a hole in his heart the size of his son. Now he's a new man. I can see it in his eyes. That's good news, honey. I'm not going to look this gift horse in the mouth." She tapped the tattoo on her arm. "The one thing I learned on the knife circuit is not to live in fear.

Trust that you'll be able to adapt to what comes next." Then she busied herself with the next customer.

I found Anita's endorsement of Paul less than ringing, but she clearly wasn't going to worry about any of my concerns. For the time being, there was nothing I could do. But while she rang up the next order, I took out a Sharpie from the pen drawer by the cash register and wrote on a blank piece of paper: "Smile! Our security cameras are filming you." I drew an arrow ambiguously pointing up. Then I taped it to the front door.

By three, Sitan still hadn't come in for work and Anita had to leave. She had a doctor appointment for the tendonitis in her wrists, she said. I told her that I could man the shop all by myself, no problem, even though deep down I was still a little afraid. After she left, I tried to console myself. Maybe now that business had picked up, Uncle would stop volunteering all over town and come back to work, or else hire somebody else to work in the shop. I tried to look on the upside. If Ma ever found out that I'd come to visit Uncle, she'd worry about whether I'd pitched in and helped or if I had been a layabout. I wouldn't want her to be ashamed.

As the sun was setting, the air grew noticeably cooler and a wind picked up, blowing dust and sagebrush and bits of trash across the parking lot. Clouds gathered along the horizon, so that the rays of the setting sun formed waves of deep red and gold, like blood trapped in amber. I looked out the window, up at the roiling sky, and thought it might actually rain. So much for it always being sunny in California. The wind picked up tiny rocks and threw them against the glass. The change in weather thinned the crowd, so by five, as the sky darkened, I could close on time. I watched the headlights creeping down the street, the traffic slower than usual, everyone inching home, heads down against the wind.

I was mopping up when the first clap of thunder shook the glass in the windows. The boom was so loud that it sounded like a truck had hit a car somewhere. I peered out the front window, expecting to see twisted metal and headlights careening across the parking lot, but instead there was a flash of lightning revealing the traffic, the parking lot, the palm trees swaying in the wild wind.

The thunder boomed again, and the rain fell all at once, as if every cloud had a little trapdoor inside, all of which opened simultaneously to release a river of water. The rain pounded onto the asphalt, splashed against the window glass, swept over the cars.

The phone rang. It was Uncle, calling to see if I was okay. He sounded genuinely worried. I was surprised that rain was such a big deal, but he said there was flooding in the canyon, whatever that meant. He said, "There will be accidents. It's like a blizzard here when it rains." He wanted me to stay put until he could get there. He'd be late, he said, but he'd drive me home. I shouldn't venture on the bus. Not in this weather.

I looked out into the blurry parking lot, the headlights reflected in the rain pouring down the glass. "I'll wait. Don't worry." He hung up, and I went back to cleaning up the shop.

Then the power went out. First the lights flickered, and then the freezer made this slow knocking sound, whined, and was suddenly silent. I stood in the middle of the front room, the world outside suddenly darker, too. All the streetlights were out, as well as the Christmas lights at the strip mall. I hadn't realized how I'd grown used to their blinking in the night air until now that they were gone and I was staring into the dark, the headlights on the street suddenly brighter and slower, unfocused-seeming, like glowing myopic eyes.

A huge clap of thunder followed, then lightning flashed across the entire sky. I saw the stark outline of the palms, their spiky leaves pointed at the dark clouds in accusation. The metal skeletons of the dark streetlamps seemed as forlorn as dandelion stems with their white seeds blown clear away. Another quick flash and its rolling peal of thunder made me feel like the earth was opening up, ready to swallow us all.

Then I saw two figures standing before the window, their faces pressed to the glass, peering inside, the whites of their eyes catching the light.

I shrieked.

Everything was black again. The two figures were still standing at the front window, rattling the door, pounding on the glass, trying to break inside.

I dropped to the floor and scurried behind the counter so they couldn't see me. I should call the police, I thought. Two holdups in a row was serious. I crept toward the phone on the wall, but then I couldn't remember if I'd checked the back door, if I'd locked it after Anita had taken the trash to the dumpster. My heart leaped to my throat. It would take forever for the police to arrive. It would be too late if the gang members got inside.

I ran to the kitchen, which was completely black. I bumped against the counter, the stool, the metal fan. I tripped over a garbage can and jammed a finger against the wall. I patted my way with both hands toward the back door until I made sure it was locked, then felt my way up the wooden frame till I could find the deadbolt, and turned that, too. Then, carefully walking in baby steps, I made my way back to the front room so I could call the cops.

I was feeling for the phone on the wall when the lights hummed and spluttered. Flat white light flooded the front room as the lights in the parking lot burst back on like little fireworks sparking in the night sky. The freezer hummed back to life. Then the zombies at the front door burst inside.

I gasped.

It was Paul and a stranger. Was this part of the plan? Casing us out this morning. Now he was back for the actual robbery.

"I called the cops!" I shouted. "They'll be here any minute!"

"You shoulda called the power company," he said nonchalantly. He shut the door carefully behind him, ushering his friend to the booth. "Cops won't do any good."

"There's no money. Anita took it with her."

"I don't need any money." Paul looked at me strangely. "What's wrong with you?" He brushed past me to grab paper towels from the roll behind the counter.

"Oh, little sister, did you think we were going to hold you up?" A deep, throaty voice spoke up from the booth, then laughed. "Bang, bang!"

I peered round Paul's shoulder. The person in the booth had long bleached-blond hair pulled back in a tight, low ponytail. I realized it was the woman from this morning. Her makeup had run in the rain, and raccoonlike pools of black mascara puddled beneath her eyes. She dabbed at her face with the paper towels Paul handed her. "Thanks, babe." Then she batted her eyes at him.

"How'd you get in? You didn't break the door, did you?"

"My father gave me a key," Paul said haughtily. "I just couldn't see to get it in the lock at first."

"Poor thing. She thought we were going to rob her." Paul's girlfriend laughed again. "We didn't mean to scare you."

"Why didn't you call first? Why did you come and then disappear like that? What's wrong with you?" I asked angrily. I didn't think it was funny the way they'd treated me.

"Half his church group was here," Paul growled. "What did you expect?"

"Of course they're here! They're so happy for him. They think it's a miracle you've come back and he's found you. This place is practically a shrine. If you'd stayed, everyone would've wanted to touch the hem of your jacket." I hadn't expected that to come out sounding as bitter as it did, but once I'd spoken, I couldn't take the words back.

Paul inhaled sharply, then blew the air out over his teeth, slowly, as though I were testing his patience, as though I were the one inconveniencing him.

Then his friend sashayed over, took some napkins from the dispenser, and began patting Paul's hair dry. "It's okay, babe. You know what's right."

With most of her makeup gone and her hair pulled back from her face, I could get a better look at Paul's girlfriend. In the unflattering fluorescent light, she looked tired, shadows under her eyes. Her skin was uneven, acne-pocked, and her jaw was sharp and determined as she wiped Paul's face dry. Her hands were really large.

And then I got it.

Paul's friend wasn't a woman.

"Oh," I said, then shut my mouth.

I turned away once then turned back toward them. Suddenly, Paul's hesitancy to introduce his friend to the church crowd made more sense.

I wondered if Uncle knew, but as soon as I asked myself the question, I knew that he didn't. My heart beat faster. I felt afraid.

"I'm Arun," the friend said, extending his hand to me to shake.

I wiped my sweaty palms on my jeans and shook Arun's hand. "Nea."

"My cousin," Paul said.

"You look so familiar," Arun said, "but I don't remember anyone named Nea."

"It's my American name."

"She's Sourdi's younger sister," Paul said.

"Sourdi! I remember her! Such a pretty little girl. She used to play at your house all the time, before it became too dangerous, moving around in the city. I remember her. Where is she now?"

"Married. Three kids. Lives in Iowa."

"Wonderful!" said Arun. "I'm so happy."

"Paul told us how you two survived."

"We were very lucky. Very, very lucky. I always thank Buddha we survived. And my big brother." Arun squeezed Paul's arm.

I wasn't sure if Arun wanted me to consider him a man or a woman. His mannerisms were feminine, his voice softer than a man's. But without his makeup and with his hair slicked back, in his blue jeans and jacket, he looked distinctly male. I wondered if this was part of the plan, a way of introducing Arun to Uncle, or if it was merely an accident of the storm. I wondered if it was bad of me to even wonder.

"I'm so pleased Paul has found his father again. The family reunited. It's like a dream come true," Arun said. "And then to meet a cousin!"

"Did you find any of your family?" I asked.

Arun shook his head. "No. I heard what happened, though, from other survivors. My mother died under Pol Pot. In one of the work camps. My father never even made it to a camp. He was killed en route. What could he do? He wore glasses. He had light skin. He looked like an intellectual. How could he hide from those brutal tyrants?"

"I'm sorry."

Arun paced in the small space between the booth and the counter, patting at his hair with one of the napkins. "They're in a better place. They're in Heaven. Or they've been reincarnated.

Maybe they're darling little babies right now while we're standing here talking about them."

Thunder rattled the glass again, but it wasn't as loud as before. The storm was finally moving on.

"Would you like something to drink? A soda? A bottle of water?" I rummaged in the refrigerated case. "I already emptied the tea and coffee pots, but we have bottled ice tea."

"Thank you for your thoughtfulness, but I'm fine." Arun sat in the booth. Arun had excellent manners, spoke in a formal Khmer, the grammar impeccable. Watching Arun sit gracefully, legs crossed, I decided I'd think of her as a woman. It seemed to fit. At least for now. She put her arms across the tabletop and lay her head down, her long hair fanning out around her so that I couldn't see her face, couldn't read her expression.

"Is Arun okay?" I whispered to Paul.

"Yeah, Arun's just tired. We had a long drive today." Paul grabbed a bottle of Coke out of the refrigerator case and opened it on the edge of the counter, popping the top off quickly. It spun on the floor like a top. He didn't bother to pick it up.

Still the rich man's son, acting like he expected servants to pick up after him. I tried not to let my irritation show.

"So when's my father coming back?" He downed a big gulp of the Coke and then belched.

"Disgusting," I said.

He smiled. "Sorry. I haven't eaten yet today."

"You were in earlier. You should have bought a donut or something."

"I didn't want to cut in line." Paul winked.

"You should be more considerate. Uncle's been waiting for you all weekend."

"I had to find Arun."

"How come you didn't know where Arun was?"

"We had a fight—"

"It's okay, babe," Arun said from the booth. Then she said in carefully enunciated English, "'Let bygone be bygone.'"

"I don't even know what that means," Paul said. His voice tacked toward anger, as though they were on the verge of picking up where the last fight ended. My body tightened, the air in the room growing tense.

The phone rang, the loud *br-r-ring* startling me.

It was Anita. "Don't panic, honey. It's going to be okay."

"What happened?"

"I don't want you to get upset now. We don't want that. That's why I waited to call you—"

"Waited to tell me what? What's going on?"

"Your uncle's going to be fine. I've been talking to the doctors—"

"Anita, what happened?!" I tried to keep my voice calm and level, but her coyness was maddening. I was squeezing the receiver so hard that I wouldn't have been surprised if it had broken in two.

"Your uncle's had a small heart attack."

"Oh, my god."

Paul and Arun were staring at me now.

"It's okay, it's—"

"It's not okay if he's had a heart attack! Which hospital? Where are you?"

I took down the name and address, then hung up. I turned to Paul. "Your car's here, right? You've got to drive us to Sacred Heart. Right now. Uncle's had a heart attack."

Paul was calmer than I would have expected. "It's going to be okay. The critical part is getting to the hospital in time."

I didn't ask him how he knew that, how he was suddenly an expert. All I could think of was Uncle working around the clock, popping his Sudafed, drinking all that caffeine, chewing the Nicorette. I should have seen this coming. I should have guessed this would come to a bad end. If he died, Ma would never forgive me. She'd think I caused it. She'd think I stressed him out.

And maybe she would be right. I was the one who thought the donut shop needed more business. Maybe I was stupid. Maybe I was wrong. Why did I have to come and confront him, make him remember the past, make him remember me?

My guilty thoughts circled round and round like a ring of smoke, all my good intentions like so many ashes. I couldn't concentrate on what Arun was saying in the car. Something about her father being a doctor. She remembered something something something. I watched the raindrops slide down the windshield and listened to the squeak of the wipers, while my heart went *boomboomboom* in my chest.

If Uncle died, it would be all my fault.

In the hospital, I had to spell his name three times and then give his American name before the woman at the registration computer finally found him in Intensive Care. They said we couldn't all go up, and I said that we were his children. The nurse looked us over, squinting. At first I was afraid she'd say we didn't look like siblings, or, worse, that she'd make us offer proof, but in the end she just nodded, buzzed us through the security door, and told us that the elevator was down the hall and to the left.

We wandered through a maze of white hallways under flickering fluorescent lights, past white walls the color of mourning, of death, of ghosts. All I could think was that I'd waited too long. I'd come all this way to see my father, to ask him why he hadn't wanted me as a daughter anymore, and I'd foolishly wasted all this time. I should have said to him straight up, first thing off the bus, I'm sorry I didn't recognize you at first, can you tell me what you remember about our family?

As we stepped out of the elevator, I saw Anita talking to a nurse at the far end of the hall. She looked wan and tired, but she wasn't crying, and she wasn't distraught. I took that as a good sign. I figured she'd look worse if Uncle wasn't going to make it.

"Anita!" I called. She turned and, seeing us, smiled in her friendly, easy, hippie way, but her eyes remained tense—only the corners of her lips turned up.

"Your uncle's resting," she told me. "They've got him on tranquilizers, blood thinner, and something to reduce the fever. He's going to be okay. He's tough. It's called unstable angina. A mild heart attack. Not much damage to the heart."

"Can we see him?"

The nurse looked at us. "Only immediate family."

"Oh, they're immediate family all right," Anita said, and the nurse let us follow her into his room.

"Don't talk very much. He's very tired," the nurse warned.

Holding my breath, I walked past the ugly white curtain hanging around his bed. I steeled myself, but I heard Paul inhale sharply beside me.

Uncle looked tiny and very weak lying on the flat white bed, the guardrails up to keep him in place, plastic tubes attached to his nostrils, IVs in both arms.

"Father!" Paul flung himself on his knees beside Uncle's bed and burst into tears.

Great, I thought. "Don't stress him out," I hissed.

But Uncle smiled and nodded, patting Paul on the back of his head with the hand that wasn't attached to the oxygen monitor.

"My son, my son," he said.

"Father, I'm here!" Paul cried.

"I know," Uncle whispered.

Arun wiped tears from the corners of her eyes and squeezed my arm tightly. She said, "I remember Paul's father. When I was a child, I was in awe of him. Everyone else looked up to him. I always thought of him as a giant. I thought he was six feet tall."

Paul was sniffling. I saw a tissue box on a table at the far end of the room, next to the dispenser of latex gloves and the needle disposal box with the orange "HAZARDOUS" sign on it. I grabbed some tissues and handed them to Paul. Then Uncle grabbed hold of my hand. He held me tightly. I leaned closer to him, but I couldn't make out what he was trying to say. His lips opened and shut, but no sound emerged.

The nurse came over. "You'd all better leave now. He needs his rest."

"We'll be back soon, James," Anita kissed her fingers and touched them to Uncle's cheek.

Arun helped Paul, who was still crying, stand up.

I patted Uncle's hand with my free hand and he released his grip, not in a scary, final kind of way, but in a tired, I-need-to-rest way. He smacked his lips together again and I realized he was thirsty. There was a plastic pitcher of water on the stand by the bed. I swabbed his mouth out with a tiny sponge on a stick, and he seemed more content. His eyes were shut and he sank into his pillow.

The heart monitor beeped steadily, the green line marking his heart rate as strong.

I leaned over him. "It's me. It's Channary. I'm back," I whispered in Khmer.

His eyelids fluttered briefly, but he didn't answer.

I turned and left with the others.

CHAPTER 18

Tiger Girl

The hospital cafeteria was still halfheartedly decorated for Christmas. Red and green garlands were draped over the salad bar like an overgrowth of mold; an artificial tree listed in the corner, burdened with a few colored balls and a strand of broken lights; the strings of popcorn looked likely to attract rats. Construction-paper angels were taped to the walls. Children had written their wishes for gifts in their crooked halos. I read a few of the requests: Power Ranger, Princess Barbie, a gun.

We gathered up our molded plastic trays and let the cafeteria ladies slop mashed potatoes and grayish meat topped with murky vegetables onto our plates, then found a table amidst all the families huddled over their grim meals.

The general atmosphere could not have been more depressing, but I felt giddy, buoyant, as though I'd plunged off a cliff only to be miraculously saved from hitting bottom. Uncle had survived, and he looked better than I'd expected. He'd wanted to hold my hand. And he hadn't seemed fazed to meet Arun. Of course, he was heavily medicated, but still. At this moment, things were looking up.

"Before he's released, we should tell the doctors that Uncle works too hard. He isn't getting any sleep. He won't listen to us, but he might listen to them if they tell him to take it easy." I wrote a checklist in my mind of things we should tell the doctors. Like all the uppers he took in a given day.

No one else seemed to share my sense of urgency. Paul was pushing the gloppy mashed potatoes around on his tray glumly, Arun picked at the dry turkey, Anita wasn't eating at all.

"So, Anita, what was Uncle doing before the heart attack? Was he volunteering at the church again? Had he picked up anything heavy? Were there any signs?" Everyone was probably still in shock, but I knew if we didn't tell the doctors these things, Uncle never would.

"Oh, I knew it was serious. He was just covered in sweat, couldn't move, it wasn't like him to complain." Anita pressed her lips together and nodded. "Thank god I only live ten minutes from the hospital. Less than ten minutes. If the ambulance hadn't come right away, I would have driven him myself."

Paul leaned forward. "What exactly was my father doing with you?"

The sharpness to Paul's tone made me look up from my tray. Anita was blushing a deep scarlet.

"Uncle's a workaholic, Paul," I said. "Don't blame Anita. It's not her fault. He was this way even in Nebraska."

"I'm not blaming anybody," Paul said through gritted teeth. "I just think I have a right to know what's going on with my father."

I didn't like his possessiveness. "You were the one who just disappeared without telling Uncle where you were going. He was worried about *you*. That was a lot of stress on him!"

"Are you blaming me now?" Paul smirked. "That's funny."

"Don't fight, please." Anita pressed her palms together.

"She's right," said Arun. "You both are worried. No need to argue."

Anita sighed. I thought she was going to try to brush off our questions, change the subject, but she surprised me.

"I have a confession. He didn't want you to know, but it's going to come up. You're his family after all. I don't want to keep secrets from you." She paused, rubbing the tattoo on her forearm. Then she plunged ahead, "We were at my place. I'd wanted him to wait out the storm. Then one thing led to another. You know how these things go. Nothing seemed out of the ordinary, until suddenly he changed color. Turned dark red. He said he couldn't breathe." Anita turned her flaming cheeks toward the wall. "He was embarrassed, he didn't want me to call an ambulance, but I told him they've seen worse."

Arun and Paul exchanged glances. Arun smiled slyly. Paul looked away. He looked embarrassed, and a little angry.

Then I realized what the blush meant. Uncle had been with Anita, as in making love with Anita. I felt the heat rising to my cheeks. I tried to push the thought of them together out of my mind, but now it was all I could think of.

It dawned on me that Uncle hadn't been working around the clock, supervising the bakers every night, as I had thought. The Kasim sisters were capable of supervising any of the new refugees they were training. All this time Uncle had been going over to Anita's place. He just hadn't wanted to tell me. "Oh, my god," I said aloud.

Anita blushed even deeper. Paul shook his head as though he wished he could shake the idea out of his ears. I didn't know what to say anymore. I pressed my Coke to the side of my face, something to soothe my burning cheeks.

A terrible thought came to me. Had Anita and Uncle been seeing each other when Auntie was alive? I'd seen Ma kiss Uncle once in the kitchen when I was eleven. I think Auntie had known that Ma had fallen in love with him. Auntie couldn't love him anymore, but she was still possessive. She hadn't wanted any woman to replace her. I had been naive to think Uncle could have turned off his heart just because he moved away from Ma, just because Auntie had turned off hers. I should have known there would be another woman.

I tipped some ice into my mouth and chewed on the cubes, concentrating on the burn inside my cheeks. I crunched down on the ice, letting the sensation of cold seep into my blood.

It was Arun who broke the uncomfortable silence that had settled over the table.

"We haven't been introduced." Arun offered a hand to Anita. "I've known the family since I was a child. Paul and I were best friends in elementary school in Phnom Penh. I'm Arun Chey."

"Anita Powell. Nice to meet you." Anita shook Arun's hand gratefully. "What a reunion this month is turning out to be! First Nea, then Paul, now you." She smiled warmly. "So do you remember Nea?"

"I didn't know any Nea. Paul told me she was Sourdi's sister." Arun turned to me, eyeing me carefully. "Funny thing is, you don't look like Sourdi. I remember her. She wore her hair in two long braids, like this." Arun gestured down her back gracefully. "But you look just like Auntie Sopheam. Isn't it funny, Paul? Your cousin looks just like your mother."

I swallowed.

"I would have guessed you were Channary if I hadn't known better," said Arun.

I stood up abruptly. No one had called me by that name since I was four.

"You sure remember a lot about our family," I said, my mouth dry, my throat constricting.

"Are you all right, Nea?" Anita asked.

"I'm thirsty. I'm going to get a refill of my Coke." I grabbed my plastic cup and headed to the soda dispenser, my back to the table so that no one would be able to read my face.

I didn't know why it scared me to hear Arun speak about the past, my past, a past I couldn't remember. I hadn't imagined that someone else on this earth might recognize me for the person I'd once been, for a member of the family I'd once been part of.

I filled my soda glass, but when I tried to drink, the liquid tasted like bile on my tongue. I dumped the soda out and filled my glass with water and ice and pressed it to the side of my face.

When I returned to our table, everyone was laughing. Arun's cheerful banter had set them at ease. The past seemed a more comfortable subject for them. Only I was terrified.

"Nea, I remember your aunt very well," Arun said. "She was a very nice lady. Very beautiful. The most elegant manners. She invited me to go along with the family to see the royal ballet at the palace. I'll never forget this experience. All the perfect little dancers like angels. And your aunt like a queen herself, dressed in a silk gown. People turned to stare at her, she was that beautiful. I felt so proud sitting next to her. I would have given anything to have seen her again."

"I saw Auntie in America," I said slowly, my heart pounding in my ears. The past as I remembered it was a minefield— growing up, when anyone would mention something about the past, I never knew if it would make the adults around me furious or sad, if they'd fall into a rage, fight with each other or me, or if they'd sink into despair, refusing to speak at all. Their moods were terrifying. I turned to Arun, tried to focus, think of something innocuous to say. I decided to start with the simplest facts. "For nine months or so, when I was eleven, we all lived together in one house in Nebraska. We'd been living in Texas, Ma and Sourdi and me and the little kids. The Baptists sponsored us. But then Uncle found us through the Red Cross, and he invited us to come live with them. Run 'the family business' together. He'd borrowed a lot of money and bought a Chinese restaurant in this small town in Nebraska. The Silver Palace. He wanted us to come work there."

Both Arun and Paul turned to me, their faces eager and open as children's.

I swallowed. Looking at them, I knew I couldn't tell them about the damaged woman I had met, scarred inside and out. I took a deep breath. "I remember Auntie would stand in the doorway, watching the wind blow in the fields. 'The wind here is uncivilized,' she would say. She couldn't speak much English, but if the customers couldn't understand her, she'd speak to them in French and say the problem was that their French was terrible."

Arun laughed. "Yes, yes! She was so elegant! That sounds just like her."

"She used to watch the soap operas every afternoon. She repeated the lines after all the characters. She said it was for our benefit, so we'd lose our 'Texas accents.' Once she caught me throwing rocks at some white boys who'd tried to attack me and the little kids in the parking lot. She was horrified. She said I was becoming an American."

All my memories made Paul and Arun laugh. At the time, when I was eleven, none of this had seemed funny. I'd found Auntie to be a harsh and bitter person, but now, in the retelling, she seemed almost heroic, fighting against the daily humiliations she faced.

"She had a picture of the family in a silver frame. Black and white. A formal portrait taken in a photography studio in Phnom Penh. She'd carried it folded up in the hem of her clothes, hiding it from the soldiers so they wouldn't know how rich she'd once been. She looked like a movie star. Her face was round and white like the moon. She looked very proud. You were in the photo, too, Paul. You stood right by Uncle."

Paul's eyes were wet. Arun put a hand on his shoulder.

"Do you have the photo?" Paul asked.

"No. Auntie kept it. I looked in Uncle's apartment, but I didn't see it there either."

Paul nodded, disappointed.

That evening, after we left the hospital and said good-bye to Anita, Paul drove us to a video store and checked out some action movies to take our minds off our troubles. Going back to the apartment without Uncle, knowing he was lying in his thin cotton gown in his cold, white hospital room, made us feel too sad and lonely to face his empty apartment for the night. We got Jiffy Pop popcorn and stopped by a liquor store and bought a couple of six-packs of beer. Paul tipped the haggard-looking man in the Santa suit ringing a bell over a red kettle on the sidewalk underneath the Budweiser sign.

Driving up and down El Camino Boulevard, we compared the garish Christmas lights that blinked on the storefronts in the shapes of flying reindeer and sleighs and obese snow-men, their colors reflected in the puddles on the sidewalks and asphalt. The rain had finally stopped, but the wind buffeted the car, gusting so that the palm trees waved wildly, their dark leaves silhouetted against the sky, the bright moonlight falling to earth like snow.

Anita had said she'd call the Kasim sisters so they wouldn't come in to work. They could call the girls they were training. We'd decided not to open the donut shop tomorrow, not without Uncle. It seemed inappropriate. As though we were going on without him, when he was the only reason all of us were here in the first place.

That night after we'd watched all three movies, each noisier and more mindless than the last, Paul and Arun fell asleep on the floor in front of the TV, but I couldn't sleep. I paced quietly from one end of the small apartment to the other, imagining them living here with Uncle. If he could still accept them when he wasn't medicated, he'd have two sons to help him and keep him company. Or maybe a son and a daughter, eventually. There was even less reason for me to stay. And I didn't feel as though I belonged.

I didn't remember Uncle as my father, the way Paul did. I didn't even remember the things Arun had shared. Arun loved those memories, but they were someone else's stories to me, nothing that I could cherish, not now, not after everything that had happened.

My family was in Nebraska, my mother the woman who had raised me as far back as I could remember, my siblings the sisters and brother I'd lived in the work camps with and crossed the minefields with and survived in the refugee camps alongside. The family I came to America with had supplanted any memory of the family I was born into. Instead my head was crowded with memories of the six of us—Ma and Sourdi, Sam and the twins and me—working and laughing and fighting together, day in, day out. I knew then that I should go home in time for the New Year. I'd make sure Uncle was okay, but I could see clearly now that what I had been seeking wasn't here in California.

What I needed wasn't the past. I didn't yearn for all the old stories anymore, not of my family and all we lost in the war, not even the ones Ma liked to tell of magical dancing girls and goddesses and all the tragic humans who tried to defy the gods and died. I didn't want to hear about the poor fools who tried to ride a crocodile and drowned, who bowed before tigers and were eaten, who ran away into a forest and turned into birds. I wanted a new story. The girl who tamed a tiger and learned how to roar. The daughter who rode a bus and reunited her grateful relatives. The student who went back to college and got her degree with honors.

From the window of Uncle's kitchen, I watched the sun rise, the edges of the sky turning pink like the inside of a shell.

The streetlights switched off, and the world was revealed, as though the night were a great tide ebbing, the inky water receding as the palm trees caught the light and glowed gold in the sun. The fronds swayed gently as sparrows darted across the sky, welcoming the morning. I slid open the window and dipped my hand into the sunlight, felt the warmth settle on my palm like a hummingbird. Leaning my elbows on the sill, I stuck my head out into the light and let the wind fill my mouth. "Roar," I said. "ROAR!"

PART SEVEN

The tiger depends upon the forest; the forest depends upon the tiger.

—traditional Cambodian proverb

CHAPTER 19

The Family Banquet

After Uncle was released from the hospital, everyone divided the work at the donut shop. Sitan said he could help with the baking at night, and Anita decided to train some more girls to work the front counter. For the first time, Uncle's business was actually being run in a way that would make it profitable, instead of just serving as a penance for his guilt-wracked soul. Paul tried to talk Uncle into expanding, opening something upscale in a larger city, but before he would consider it, Uncle said there was something more urgent that he needed to do first. He wanted Paul and me to visit Auntie's grave.

She was buried in a mausoleum in a cemetery on the outskirts of town. "It's pretty. Your mother liked it," Uncle told Paul in the car.

"Auntie picked out her cemetery?" I exclaimed.

"For both of us," Uncle said. "She knew her health was poor."

We drove through the tall black wrought-iron gates and circled past row after row of grave markers, the bright sunlight incongruously cheerful. The far side of the cemetery had fancy crosses and giant pavilions, but the area we drove toward was more modest, with flat markers, easy to mow over, and a copse of young cypress trees casting thin tendrils of shade over the graves. We parked on the side of the asphalt and walked across the browning winter lawn toward the stone mausoleum. I tried to read the names on the graves as we passed. There was an Armacost, a Miller, a Garcia, a Lopez, then a Lee and some Chinese symbols, a Mozelewski, and a Mueller. A young girl's grave was marked with pinwheels and a teddy bear. A woman who'd died in her teens decades ago had fresh yellow roses.

Inside the mausoleum, Uncle led us down the center aisle, then turned left and stopped three spaces in. He pointed, and I saw Auntie's name in gold calligraphy: Sopheam Chhouen, written in American style, with her personal name first and Uncle's surname. Uncle's name was next to hers, the year of his death left blank. Khmer script ran beneath the English, looking elegant and final.

The black-and-white photograph of the family had been set into the marble tablet alongside her name in English and Khmer. I was shocked to see it again. I peered closer. The last time I'd seen it was in Auntie's room, and I had barely glanced at the little girl in the picture. Now I stared at myself. My expression was exactly like Auntie's, our lips set in identical half-curls, slightly mocking, a little haughty. When I was eleven, I hadn't recognized these people, my family, they'd seemed like alien creatures, but now I could clearly see that Uncle and Paul had the same cheekbones, the same long noses and straight lips. Their younger selves stared back at us calmly.

Paul stood before the photograph, tracing the outline of Auntie's face with his finger. Then he stepped back, bowed three times before the placard, and knelt on the cold floor.

Uncle put his hand on Paul's shoulder. "I have found our son," Uncle addressed the tomb in Khmer. "I promised you I would find him and I have. Our eldest son, Ponleu. I hope that you can rest now. I will take care of your son until I am reunited with you. I am sorry that I failed you in life, but I have fulfilled your last wish. We will come to your grave every year. We will bring you incense and sweet fruit, we will never forget you." Then Uncle bowed three times before her grave as well.

I followed him, but I didn't know what to say aloud. I closed my eyes, and thought, "I'm sorry I disappointed you, Mother." But that seemed false and hypocritical. To whom was I actually praying? And why say things I didn't mean? I touched the placard, ran my fingers along the gold lettering. Then I stepped back and whispered, "You were very brave. I'll always remember you." And I bowed.

When I turned around again, I thought Uncle was crying. His eyes were shut tightly, but when he opened them again, I saw they were bright and shining. Uncle did not look sad so much as hopeful.

Before we left, Uncle pressed his hand to the picture embossed on the marble and stroked the photograph gently.

As we left the mausoleum, blinking in the sunlight, the world unnaturally bright and calm, Paul stepped away. His face was flushed, his emotions still turbulent. He said he had to make a call, he'd seen a pay phone by the front gate. I assumed he wanted to talk to Arun. Clearly he needed to share his thoughts with someone he knew and trusted. That wouldn't be Uncle or me. We might be family, but we were all essentially strangers.

Uncle and I walked back to the car alone and waited, leaning against the Toyota.

Uncle stared at me. "You look so much like her," he said, but not as sadly as he had when I'd first arrived in California. He nodded. "It's good. She would have been so proud to see you like this. The first member of the family to go to college in America. A beautiful young woman."

I didn't know what to say. "Thank you."

Then Uncle paused. "There's something I should tell you."

My heartbeat quickened. I'd been telling myself all this time that this was exactly what I'd wanted to hear, what I'd wanted him to acknowledge, but now, in this moment, I felt afraid. I didn't know why. My heart pounded in my chest, drummed in my ears. My body broke out in a cold sweat. I realized then that I was afraid he'd ask me to stay in California with him and Paul, and, truth be told, I didn't want to. I wanted to go back home to see my family, the family I knew and loved, the family who had raised me. And, quickly, I tried to brace myself, tried to think of a polite way to tell him no without hurting his heart.

"I already know," I said quickly. "Sourdi told me. I know you are my father, I know Auntie is my mother. She told me before I went to college."

"I wasn't sure until the hospital." And I knew then that he'd heard me call myself Channary. Uncle swallowed. "Your mother was so happy to find you alive." I must have looked surprised or skeptical, despite my efforts to keep my face blank, to show nothing. I was too nervous, I didn't trust my emotions. But now Uncle put his hand on my shoulder. "She could see you were smart. We could all see that. When we left for California, she wanted to take you with us, but I thought we should wait. Wait until you were older. She was ill, and you were so happy where you were. You were doing so well. How could we look after a child? We argued about this. Maybe I was wrong."

"No, you were right." I opened my mouth, but I didn't know if the words I was thinking actually came out. I didn't know if I could actually say what I was feeling.

Uncle rubbed his face with his hand, and I thought he would cry again, but he remained calm. "Your mother was very proud of you."

"It's Ma she didn't like," I said. Even I heard the words come flying out this time.

Uncle looked at me, startled.

"That's what Ma said."

"Sometimes it's hard between sisters. Your mother was used to being the best, the most successful, the most beautiful. It was hard for her."

I didn't tell him I knew about his feelings for Ma, that they had fallen in love, or thought they had, at least. They had broken Auntie's heart, what was left of it. It didn't matter anymore. Somehow facing him, hearing his confession, I no longer felt burdened by the old worries, the old rivalries and dramas in the family. I had feared this moment, confronting Uncle, and now here it was passing by, already becoming a story I might tell to someone else someday. Maybe Sourdi, maybe a friend, maybe my own daughter one day. The moment my father admitted I was his daughter. The moment I realized I didn't need anything more from him.

"It's the war," I said. "It's Pol Pot's fault."

"Yes," said Uncle. "It is."

Then we both fell into our own silences.

I told Uncle on the drive back that I was going to return to Nebraska. I wanted to try to make it for the New Year. I said I'd been very happy to see him again, but I missed everybody at home. He said he understood, and then insisted upon taking me out to eat at a fancy Chinese restaurant he liked closer to L.A., off the 5 in the San Gabriel Valley. It was huge, two stories, with several banquet rooms. I'd never seen a Chinese restaurant like this, not even in Dallas. Each floor was packed with families celebrating the holidays, the noise level deafening. As we crowded into the waiting room, I thought we might stand out, I worried people might stare, the way people used to stare at us when we first moved to Nebraska. At least we were a big group, strong enough to assert ourselves: Uncle, Anita, Sitan (wearing his daughter in the Snugli around his neck), Paul and

Arun, who had her hair down, looking very glamorous, and me. But no one even gave us a second glance. Every family was its own island, busy with its own concerns. There were elderly grandparents in wheelchairs or pushing walkers, their grown kids helping them navigate through the maze of tables while hyper children raced around the edges. There were families whose members put their heads down and ate in silence, barely looking at each other as they shoveled food methodically into their mouths, and families that talked and laughed and waved their chopsticks over their rice bowls, barely touching their food. There were happy parents and harried parents, bored teenagers, angry infants, sleeping babies, squawling babies, laughing grandparents, grandparents slumped asleep in their chairs. There was every iteration of family, including our table.

Uncle tried to order a lot of expensive dishes, the kind with shellfish and high cholesterol, but Anita took over the menu and insisted upon "heart healthy" dishes. The kind with lots of vegetables and no flavors, Uncle said dismissively.

"You don't want to end up back in the hospital," Anita said, taking charge.

Uncle shook his head.

"It's funny. I thought only fat people had heart attacks," Sitan said.

When the dishes came out, Uncle seemed disappointed, no matter how much the rest of us oohed and ahhed and exclaimed over the delicate flavors, the clay pot stew of mushrooms and fungus, the chow fun with black bean sauce, sticky rice, fish dumplings, the glistening baby bok choy, the platters of spinach and squash, the winter melon soup. I couldn't tell if Uncle was genuinely missing meat or if he was being polite, apologizing for bounty, playing the good host.

Eating like this felt decadent, but it also felt like a true celebration. Paul and Arun and I could all remember days when we'd eaten insects, vermin, leaves, stones, maggots, dead things we found, and strange, small things we captured and killed, just to stay alive. Eating a true banquet together felt like a dream, like a miracle. Once upon a time, I would have felt afraid, wondering when our luck would turn, when the next bad thing would happen to balance out the good. I would have clenched my stomach and hunched my shoulders instead of eating my fill, as if I could ward off the pain of life's next blow. But this evening, seeing Uncle smile, watching my brother and his partner, alive and in love, seeing Sitan tempt his daughter with delicious foods on the end of a glass spoon, noticing Anita sneak a loving glance Uncle's way, I didn't feel afraid, I felt warm and happy. I knew this feeling wouldn't last forever; it might not even last a full day. Sometimes a moment of happiness here and there was all any of us got, but I also knew that any unhappiness wouldn't have to be permanent either. For the first time, I felt as though I could handle what life threw at me. I felt confident I'd find a way.

After another round of chrysanthemum tea, I excused myself to go to the ladies room. I wove through the round tables of Chinese families, past the waiters carrying trays laden with tureens and platters and plates on one arm like they weighed nothing, around the women wielding their carts of dim sum through the crowded dining room like war chariots, and all the way to the very back, where the fish tanks weren't just for show or feng shui but for holding the evening's special "Catch of the Day." I saw my reflection in the dark mirror behind the bar, my startled face peering back at me from among the liquor bottles and dusty glasses and jars of colored swizzle sticks. Then I turned and looked over my shoulder at all the tables of families eating, celebrating birthdays and reunions and Little League victories and the other mundane occasions that brought the generations together to eat in public, to display their solidarity in being a family, all the arguments and disagreements and secrets and pain temporarily tucked away from public view. I saw Uncle smiling as Sitan discussed something animatedly with Arun, Anita and Paul leaning their heads close as they conferred, and I realized that they looked like any other family here—whole, despite wars and losses and crossing oceans. They didn't look mismatched. They looked like they belonged together.

It was me who didn't belong, but I didn't feel bad about that anymore.

CHAPTER 20

Return to the Palace

Before he drove me to the bus station, Uncle handed me a plain envelope stuffed with cash. "Take it, it's your wages, don't argue," he said, pushing the envelope into my backpack. "Don't let anyone see. Don't leave it lying where they can take it, especially when you sleep."

I didn't open the envelope because that would have been rude. Instead I threw my arms around Uncle's neck and hugged him good-bye. "I'll use this for my books," I said.

"I will help you with your college," he said.

"It's okay. I have a scholarship."

He squeezed me hard, then turned away so that I couldn't see his face, couldn't see that his eyes were tearing. "Maybe we can have a reunion. Tell your mother, bring the kids. For Cambodian New Year. There's a temple in Long Beach."

"They'd love to see you again. And Paul. We could celebrate," I said. "April's just around the corner."

He nodded, then wiped his face with a handkerchief. We both pretended it was just the cold air that made him blow his nose.

I'd finally made up my mind to call Ma the night before. But first, I practiced what I would tell her: that I was coming back early, I wasn't going to stay in California all winter break as I'd planned. I was terrified that the moment I opened my mouth, she'd see through me just as she had when I was growing up so I tried to come up with all the detailed questions she might ask me: where was the interview, what did they ask me, what had I worn, what did my roommate's house look like, had I remembered to thank her family? My hand was shaking as I dialed her number in the kitchen.

"Hello?" she answered on the first ring.

"Ma! It's Nea. I'm coming home early—"

"Good!" she interrupted. "You should spend the holidays with your family! I didn't want to say anything, I didn't want to make you feel bad, but really I thought, I've missed you, away in college all these months, now I won't see you." Then she shouted to the side, "Marie! Jennifer! Sam—put that down—take off your shoes—listen—Your sister's coming home!" I figured they must have just come in the door. I could see them shedding their coats, hanging them on the row of hooks we'd nailed on the wall, kicking their muddy shoes onto the mat. Then Ma told me how business was going at the Palace, the new menu she was designing, the special vegetarian entrées ("It's all they want these days! Tofu, tofu, tofu. Such a fad, you won't believe it. I remember when they only wanted meat!"), and the weather, the terrible weather, so dry this year, all the farmers were complaining, not even a white Christmas, was this the sign of another drought? The wind was fierce as ever, the clouds gathered every day, but the wind blew the snow away.

She had so much news to tell me, things she'd been bottling up, complaints she couldn't tell the younger kids, details of all the casual daily frustrations that made up her days, that I didn't have time to say any of my rehearsed speech.

"You know how that crazy Mrs. Beasel always tries to get free food—free eggroll, free dessert, wraps food in her napkin and puts it in her purse? She died. Yep, so sad."

"She didn't die in the Palace, did she?"

"No, of course not. I read it in the paper."

Finally there was a crash in the background and the sound of my sisters' voices rising in fury, a flurry of calls for her intervention, "Mom! Mommy!" And my mother said she had to go, but she was glad I'd called. "It's good you're coming home early. Your sisters are going to drive me crazy," she said, and then she hung up.

My heart leapt to my throat and stayed there. She had missed me, I realized. She really did care that I'd been gone.

The bus ride across Nevada seemed endless, especially after the on-bus toilet broke again, but by the time we reached Utah, I was literally pushing against the floor of the bus with my feet, as though I could will it to go faster, as though wishing could make something true.

I had decided I would admit to Ma what I had done. Very simply. I'd say, I'm sorry I lied, but I went to California to see Uncle. Before she could get angry, I'd tell her the good news, that we'd found Uncle's oldest son, alive and well. A miracle. Imagine all of us together for the New Year, I'd say. Wouldn't that be something to celebrate? Such good luck after all these years. I figured her happiness would take the edge off her anger. As far as telling her that I'd found out who I was, I'd save that for later, for my next confession.

As I watched the flat fields pass by, I thought about the new story I would have to weave, a story that could encompass all of us, the whole family. How once upon a time we were lost, scattered, afraid. We wandered in the jungle, we flew over the sea, we fought in the streets, we worked in hostile villages and unfriendly cities, until, battered and bruised, we lost the power to see. Like the Apsaras who fell from Heaven, we could not recognize our own faces. Then slowly by slowly, we found each other, one by one, the family came together, only to discover we'd forgotten how to speak. We called out like the sisters who'd turned into birds, our words mere sounds, animal cries, nothing we could understand. But then we struggled harder and taught ourselves to speak again, one word at a time in our new American voices, until we could roar with the tigers. We were creating a new story, one about a family with a happy ending.

The first flakes of snow began to fall as we passed the Wyoming-Nebraska border. Tiny ice chips from the tight-fisted clouds struck the windows like rice at a wedding. Downy clouds covered the sky from one end of the horizon all the way to Iowa, the sky and the road the same shade of steel. I watched jackrabbits hopping across the empty fields, crows circling in patterns like black lace through the sky, searching for stray cobs of corn or soybean pods. The wind swept through the ditches, the bromegrass swaying like the fur of a great beast bracing its back before a storm.

A big snowstorm was coming. I imagined the world turning white, like a blank slate, erasing all the work of the past year so that we could start over fresh, so that when the first rays of sun emerged after the storm, the whole world would spark with light.

I changed buses at the intersection to the state highway, and from there it was another three and half hours home. The Greyhound left me off at the Super 8 opposite our restaurant. I recognized Ma's Honda in the parking lot in front of the Palace.

I zipped up my coat and shivered in the wind as I waited for the driver to pull my backpack from the luggage bin under the bus, and then I was running across the parking lot, squinting into the wind, the light from the Palace windows shining like beacons.

I burst through the front door, and the familiar scent of curries and stir-fry and sweet-and-sour pork and the incense that Ma burned on the shrine in the very back of the dining room filled my nostrils. I blinked, trying to see clearly. My face felt frozen. After three weeks in California I'd grown unused to the cold. There were a few families chowing down, an unfamiliar waitress serving.

Then, over the tinny cheer of the canned carols, I heard my mother's voice calling, "Nea! Nea! You're back!" Ma ran out the kitchen doors, through the dining room, and hugged me. "I think you grew taller!"

"Ma, I stopped growing in high school."

"No, you are definitely taller." Ma smiled to the family seated at a center table. "This is my daughter. She's been away at college." She squeezed my shoulders. "She's growing so tall!"

She took my arm. "Come on, I'll show you something. A surprise. Hurry now."

She pulled me toward the kitchen, and I thought, It's some new menu disaster, some fusion thing she's created, like her fried mashed potatoes with hot mustard dipping sauce or the twins' hamburger chow fun.

I stepped into the kitchen and the lights went out. I heard giggling.

Ma said, "Close your eyes."

"It's already dark," I said, but I closed my eyes.

Then the twins came out carrying a cake with sparkler candles sizzling on top.

"Surprise!" everyone shouted, and I recognized my brother Sam, the twins, the cook, Ma, and some white kid I assumed she'd hired to work in the Palace, until I realized he was holding Marie's hand and that he was probably my sister's new boyfriend, now that Ma let the girls date white guys.

"But it's not my birthday."

"It's not for your birthday," Sam said.

"It's for you," Ma said. "Dean's list. We saw your report card."

"What?"

"Yeah, it came in the mail a couple days ago," Marie said.

"You opened my report card?"

"Make a wish," Sam said. "Hurry up and blow out your candles."

"I don't think I can make a wish if it's not my birthday."

"Of course you can," Ma said.

So I closed my eyes and blew out the candles while everyone clapped, but when I opened my eyes, I realized I'd forgotten to make a wish. But that was okay, I didn't believe in wishes. Anyway, the candles sparked back to life right away, and Marie and Jennifer giggled hysterically, like the fifteen-year-olds they were. "They're trick candles!" they announced. "Got you!"

"It's okay," I said. "I already got my wish."

Ma turned the lights back on, and suddenly someone's hands covered my eyes. "Ha ha," I said, playing along. "You got me."

"I sure did!" said a familiar voice. And I realized it was my sister Sourdi. "Surprise!" she cried.

I pulled her hands away. "Sourdi! Sourdi! You're here!" I threw my arms around her shoulders. I hadn't expected to see her. Trips were so hard, what with all her kids. I hadn't seen her since I graduated from high school and visited her in Iowa. I held her tight. "You won't believe who I saw in California," I whispered.

But before she could reply, I felt little hands, like so many eager monkeys, pulling at my jeans and my sweatshirt, enlacing my legs. "We're here, too!" Sourdi's kids, my nieces and nephew, screeched happily.

"You look good," I told Sourdi, and I wasn't lying. She'd gotten her hair streaked in long blond tendrils, she was wearing a lot of makeup, but tastefully done, and she smelled like a perfume you couldn't buy in a drugstore. She looked like a grown-up, like a mother, like a woman who'd grown into herself, no longer like the girl who'd left home too soon.

"Ma called me last night. Asked if I could drive up with the kids to welcome you home. You're full of surprises, Nea."

"I would have told you I was going," I started, but then I stopped, because that was a lie, and I didn't want to lie again.

Sourdi squeezed my hand. "So Ma told me you went to find an *internship*?" She lifted an eyebrow, but she smiled too, and I knew she'd guessed my secret, and she'd already forgiven me. Sourdi had always been my best friend, my protector, and I was still her favorite. I could tell.

Ma brought out our special dessert plates and I helped cut up the cake—a special ice cream one from the Piggly Wiggly, mint chocolate chip; Ma had remembered my favorite.

"So how was California?" Sam asked. "You see any movie stars?"

"Even better," I said. "You're not going to believe what happened."

"It's no fun if you don't see movie stars," he said, and grabbed his plate. "I'm taking this upstairs, Ma. Game's on." And he rushed out.

The twins took their cake and started giggling with Marie's boyfriend, who thanked me politely when I handed him his slice. "Can we go finish watching the game, too, Ma?" the girls begged, and Ma let them go. Sourdi gathered up her children and followed the others. She paused at the door and winked at me, quickly, so only I would see.

I listened as their footsteps trooped up the back stairs like a parade of tiny royal elephants celebrating the new year.

Ma pulled up a stool next to me at the prep counter. "You can tell me. I want to hear all about your trip."

"I will, Ma. But not tonight."

"No, not tonight," Ma agreed. She put her spoon into the mint ice cream and licked it delicately. "You came home just in time. We're going to have a storm. Weatherman says maybe six inches. Let's look."

She took me by the elbow, and we walked to the back door and peeked outside. Sure enough, snow was swirling from the dark sky. We watched the flakes spiraling through the air, illuminated by the tall light in the parking lot, each flake floating gently like so many goose feathers.

"Like spring," Ma said.

"What? It's freezing!"

"It looks like the flower petals in spring. The rains come and they fall from the trees. When I was girl, I used to like to dance in the first rain. My sister and I, we'd run out under the trees and let the petals fall into our hair." Ma patted her head and stroked the air by her shoulders, imaging the long locks she used to possess. "We used to say they looked like pearls, like diamonds. We were very vain." Her eyes grew bright and moist as she thought about the past.

"Come on, Ma," I said. "Let's go! Quick, quick!"

I grabbed her by the hand and, giggling, we ran into the snow like schoolgirls ready to be bathed in flower petals.

The wind gusted and I held Ma's arm tight, so she wouldn't fall as we made our way across the icy parking lot into the pool of white light. The snow swirled around us, and we tilted our heads back to catch snowflakes on our tongues. We held out our palms, letting the crystals gather there like jewels we had skimmed from the sea of milk at the very beginning of time. We were like dancing girls witnessing the birth of the universe.

Side by side, we laughed in the falling snow.

ACKNOWLEDGMENTS

I began this story to keep a promise I made to a survivor of the Khmer Rouge. When I was fifteen, I interviewed a Sino-Cambodian woman who had moved to the small town in South Dakota where I lived with my family. I wrote features for the local paper and often interviewed people with interesting stories and backgrounds. The woman wanted to tell me how her children had died as she tried to escape the Khmer Rouge. However, after I wrote up the article, my mother told me I should not submit it to the paper. "Don't draw attention to them," she said. "They've already received threats." Then my mother told me that the woman had confided in her that people had even threatened to "fire bomb" the Cambodian family's restaurant. It was the early 1980s, and anti-Asian sentiment was high in the Midwest because of constant Japan-bashing in the media. While Cambodian refugees could not be further removed from the Japanese auto executives being vilified in the press, the differences were not apparent to local bigots terrified of the "economic Pearl Harbor" that the media warned against. Thus, I did not submit my article to the paper, but instead resigned out of frustration. Shortly thereafter, the woman moved away with her husband and American-born children. They had sold their restaurant at a loss and decided to move back to Texas, where they felt safer. I lost touch with her after she left.

Eventually, I too left that small town, for college in Grinnell, Iowa, where I formed a mentoring group for the children of Southeast Asian refugees, including the many Cambodians who had relocated to the state in the 1980s. After I graduated,

I became a reporter for the Associated Press, where I made a point of covering the Southeast Asian community, first in Des Moines, Iowa, and later in Denver, Colorado. I hoped that as a member of the media I could make a difference in a way that I had been unable to do as a teenager.

Long after I left the AP, I still felt haunted by my inability to tell the story of that first Cambodian family that I had met. Finally, I wrote the novel *Dragon Chica*, creating a young Cambodian American narrator, Nea Chhim, who could tell the story of her family's struggles in America. While I did include the story of the first refugee I ever interviewed, revealing how her children died under the Khmer Rouge, I also expanded the narrative to include the stories that I had witnessed firsthand: the stories of the first generation of Cambodian refugees to come to America in the 1980s to make a new life in this country.

I was immensely gratified that readers responded so positively to the story of Nea and her family. When my publisher, Trish O'Hare at GemmaMedia, heard that students had asked if I would write a sequel, she immediately wanted to know if I would do so. Thus, I agreed to write this novel to explore the part of the family that I had not been able to include in the first book due to the constraints of time and space.

In continuing my research for this novel, I have benefitted from many sources, including many brave and accomplished Cambodian Americans willing to share their own stories with me, retired foreign service officers, scholars, volunteers who have worked with refugees in America, as well as the work of scholars and artists who have done much to document Cambodian history—not only the Khmer Rouge era (1975–78) but other periods of Cambodia's rich and complex culture. I found these books particularly helpful: *At the Edge of the Forest: Essays on Cambodia, History, and Narrative in Honor of*

David Chandler, edited by Anne Ruth Hansen and Judy Ledgerwood (Ithaca, NY: Southeast Asia Program Publications, 2008); Elizabeth Becker, *When the War Was Over: The Voices of Cambodia's Revolution and Its People* (NY: Simon and Schuster, 1986); David Chandler, *A History of Cambodia* (Boulder, CO: Westview Press, 2000) and *Voices from S-21: Terror and History in Pol Pot's Secret Prison* (Berkeley, CA: University of California Press, 1999); *Children of Cambodia's Killing Fields: Memoirs by Survivors*, compiled by Dith Pran, edited by Kim DePaul (New Haven, CT: Yale University Press, 1997); Ben Kiernan, *The Pol Pot Regime: Race, Power, and Genocide in Cambodia Under the Khmer Rouge, 1975–1979* (New Haven: Yale University Press, 1996); Christopher Hitchens, *The Trial of Henry Kissinger* (NY: Verso, 2001); Peter Maguire, *Facing Death in Cambodia* (NY: Columbia University Press, 2005); Vibol Ouk and Charles Martin Simon, *Goodnight Cambodia: Forbidden History* (Soquel, CA: Dead Trees Are Alive Publications, 1998); Samantha Power, *A Problem from Hell: America in the Age of Genocide* (NY: Harper Perennial, 2003); Dith Pran, *Children of the Killing Field*; Sharon K. Ratliff, *Caring for Cambodian Americans: A Multidisciplinary Resource for the Helping Professions* (NY: Garland Publishing, 1997); Margaret Slocomb, *An Economic History of Cambodia in the Twentieth Century* (Singapore: National University of Singapore Press, 2010); William Shawcross, *Sideshow: Kissinger, Nixon, and the Destruction of Cambodia* (NY: Simon and Schuster, 1979); William E. Willmott, *The Chinese in Cambodia* (Vancouver: University of British Columbia Publications Centre, 1967) and *The Political Structure of the Chinese Community in Cambodia* (NY: Humanities Press, 1970).

I found the following sources useful for Cambodian proverbs: http://cambodianculture.wordpress.com/2008/03/

16/khmer-sayings/; Judith M. Jacob, *The Traditional Literature of Cambodia* (Oxford University Press, 1996), and www.khmer-institute.org.

I was also greatly helped by three films: Davy Chou's documentary on the movie industry in pre-Khmer Rouge Cambodia, *Golden Slumbers* (*Le Sommeil d'or*), 2011; the haunting documentary by Thet Sambot and Rob Lemkin, directors, *Enemies of the People*, 2009; and the political documentary by Eugene Jarecki, director, *The Trials of Henry Kissinger*, 2002. I highly recommend memoirs by the following authors for first-hand accounts of life under Pol Pot: Chanrithy Him, Loung Ung, Thida Buth Mam (written with JoAn D. Criddle), Sichan Siv, and Paul Thai.

I would like to thank Yenly Thach, Laura Tevary Mam, Ratha Kim, and Jenny Chea-Vaing for sharing personal stories as well as for their own work promoting the beauty of Cambodian culture; Dr. Stanton Jue, who was stationed as a young U.S. foreign service officer in Phnom Penh in the 1950s, for sharing with me his memories of getting to know the Chinese business community and *congrégations* (as the French had called the native-place associations), and Florence Jue, who told me vivid stories about teaching English, watching the royal ballet at the palace, and living as a diplomat's wife in Phnom Penh; Dr. Franklin Huffman, who shared with me memories of traveling throughout Cambodia in the 1960s while researching various Cambodian dialects for his dissertation; members of the Southeast Asian Arts and Culture Coalition and the Indochinese Housing Development Center for their wonderful programs and events promoting Southeast Asian and Cambodian culture in San Francisco and the Bay Area; Sandra Sengdara Siharath, founder of SEACHAMPA. org; Dr. Halleh Seddighzadeh, volunteer with the Center for Empowering Refugees and Immigrants in Oakland; Dr.

Jessica Elkind, for allowing me to audit her graduate seminar in Southeast Asian history at San Francisco State University; Dr. Scott Lankford, whose brilliant students at Foothill College first inspired this book with their probing questions and request for a sequel, including Rebecca Hoffman, Elizabeth Jug, Colin Madondo, Shervin Nakhjavan, Vivian Reed, Emily Romanko, Ksenia S., and Aigerim Zholmurzayeva; City College of San Francisco librarian Maura Garcia; East-West reading series coordinator Suzanne Lo; bookstore manager Eden Lee; and Mary Marsh of the John Adams Library. I especially want to thank friends whose encouragement was essential to this project: Jeni Fong, Howard Wong, Lynne Ewart-Felts, Timothy Ota, Walter Mason, Lorraine Saulino-Klein, Edith Oxfeld, Sheryl Fairchild, Dr. Herena Kim, Babette André, Joe McGowan, Jr., and Nina Wolff, cover model Lotus Tai; Jeff, Virginia, Ariel, Everett, Adelaide, and Evelyn for all their love and support; my father, Winberg Chai, who wields a mean red pen and is always my first editor; Jennifer Sale for her sharp-eyed and judicious copyediting; my brilliant and hardworking agent, Penn Whaling; and my inspirational editor, Trish O'Hare.

Some of the characters and events in this novel first appeared in stories in somewhat different forms in the following publications, which I would like to acknowledge: *Many Mountains Moving, Seventeen, Zyzzyva, Jakarta Post Weekender Magazine,* and my collection of short stories, *Glamorous Asians* (University of Indianapolis Press, 2004).

CPSIA information can be obtained at www.ICGtesting.com
Printed in the USA
BVOW07s2230171013

334044BV00001B/3/P

9 781936 846450